*** Chapter 1 ***

Since three a.m., Chew sat camouflaged and gripped up with his gun in the back yard of an old school hustler named Jac, sister's house. It was now 7:10 a.m. and Chew was still patiently waiting for Jac to pull up. Jac was a heavyweight in the crack game, he was getting bricks of cocaine from Texas for a low price and was easily doubling his profit back home in Buffalo, NY.

Jac was a low-key smooth hustler that managed to avoid the spotlight. Not too many people knew about him because he kept a low profile. Chew had been doing his homework on Jac and studying him for six months now. Learning his movements, stash houses, and any other places he went. Karen, Jac's sister, lived in Cheektowaga, a suburb of Buffalo, NY.

Cheektowaga is a suburb with no tolerance for criminal activity. Most of the residents felt safe resting their heads there at night. Cheektowaga was a good spot to stash drugs and money because not too many stick up kids would "play" in Cheektowaga. Karen was in her mid-forties, and worked at a nursing home taking care of the elderly. Although she received monthly payments from Jac for stashing his drugs at her house, she worked hard for everything she had and took pride in it.

Although Chew was good at doing his homework on people, he was not sure if Karen's house was really one of Jac's stash houses or not. Chew did have a gut feeling that something of Jac's was in her house, and his gut was never wrong.

After twenty minutes went by, a black Altima Nissan pulled up to Karen's driveway, catching Chew by surprise. Chew always did his homework thoroughly, he never saw Karen or Jac driving this black Altima. The car pulled up in the driveway and Karen exited the Altima wearing her work uniform. Once Chew realized it was Karen, he shook his head.

Chew was twenty-six years old and been doing home invasions and robbing drug dealers ever since he was fourteen years old. Over the years, Chew stuck to his number one rule, "No robbing regular people." Chew wasn't the type of stick up kid that would rob honest working people.

Chew would keep drug dealers and players that played the game as his targets. Chew understood that patience and good timing were two main things needed when pulling up off a lic, and right now was the perfect time to hit this lic. Chew shook his head at the thought that he would be walking Karen in the house instead of Jac. Chew was just hoping that Karen wouldn't try and fight back because if she did, then it would definitely turn into a homicide.

Karen was walking so fast to her back door that she didn't even notice the killer laying in her yard waiting for her to unlock the door. When Karen got to the door, she began roaming through her purse looking for her house keys. By the time she realized the masked man with a Glock 40 was right behind her, it was too late.

With his left hand, Chew quickly snatched Karen by the collar of her shirt and pointed his drawn gun to her face with his right hand.

"Let's not make this no muthafuckin homicide, I'm here for da shit dat Uncle Jac got up in here".

Chew said calmly and loud enough for only Karen to hear. Karen was so shaken, the pee she was holding in came running all down her legs. Once Chew saw the fear in her eyes, he knew he had her right where he wanted her.

Karen began pleading for her life.

"Please don't kill me, you could have the stuff!"

Chew looked around to make sure no neighbors were watching. "Aight, let's open up this door."

While Karen was trying to calm her nerves down, Chew had his gun pointed to the back of her head. This was the first time Karen had ever been held at gun point. Karen was praying that the masked-up man wouldn't kill her, she was so scared that her hands were shaking while she was trying to put the key in the door. Chew grabbed her hands and turned her around, through his ski mask he looked her straight in the eyes.

"Stop fuckin wasting time, get it together!"

Although, Jack felt like Karen house in Cheektowaga would be a safe stash place, he still told her what to do in case of a robbery. After feeling the chrome metal from Chew's Glock 40 rubbing against her head. Karen understood that she had to get it together before the masked-up man blew her brains out.

After unlocking the backdoor, Chew walked Karen into the back hallway and up a few stairs. Before he let Karen open the house door, he asked her was there anybody inside the house. In a shaky voice Karen said.

"No, nobody else is in there"

As soon as they got inside the house, Karen led Chew to a closet. Karen opened the closet door and kicked some clothes off a duffle bag. Chew made Karen drag the duffle bag out of the closet and open it. Inside the duffle bag was ten bricks of cocaine and ten pounds of weed. Karen looked at Chew hoping this was enough to satisfy him.

"This is what Jac got in my house."

Chew looked at Karen.

"You think I'm fucking stupid or something?"

Chew knew that those ten bricks and ten pounds were a dummy stash. Old school hustlers like Jac kept a dummy stash for situations like this, hoping that the stickup kid would be satisfied and miss out on the real stash. Chew looked Karen in the eyes.

"I been watching you and Jac for the past few weeks, I know dat Altima dat you're driving ain't ya car, and I know dat Jack got more shit in here! You got one last chance to tell me where everything is at or I'm going to blow ya brains out and just find it myself."

Chew placed his gun under Karen's chin grabbing a fist full of her hair. Karen realized that if she wanted to remain alive, she had to skip Jac's plan and give the masked man his stash.

"Okay, okay everything is downstairs in the basement"

Karen finally gave in, Chew kept his left fist full of Karen's hair, and gun in the right hand pointed to the back of her head.

"Let's go, take me to dat shit now!"

Chew was known for hitting good lics for a few bricks at the most, but when Karen showed him the duffle bags, he realized this was his biggest lic. He knew those two duffle bags full of bricks of cocaine, and two duffle bags full of weed was the rest of the stash. All he could say to himself was "Jac- Muthafuckin- Pot"

****

It's been almost three days since L had gotten some rest. For the last two days instead of bearing down on the block, L been bearing down in one of the houses he owned around the way. While sitting down on the couch counting his money, there was a knock on the front door. L gripped his 44 Bulldog Mag and walked up to the front window to see who it was. When he looked out the window, he saw that it was a smoker named Felicia. L opened the door and Felicia came into the front hallway.

"Nephew you still up?"

Felicia asked while sticking her right hand inside her bra to get her money. Felicia pulled the money out, and unfolded three wrinkled up twenty-dollar bills. L looked at Felicia.

"I'm always up, hustlers don't sleep we rest with one eye up."

Felicia looked at L while he was walking.

"I hear that."

Felicia handed L sixty dollars.

"Here Nephew dis sixty dollars, make it right for Aunty."

L took the money and walked over to the glass table in the dining room and grabbed a sandwich bag that was filled with crack. He ripped off a piece of paper from a notebook and started dumping the crack on it.

"Here you go Aunty".

L handed Felicia the piece of paper and she quickly stashed it in her bra.

"Thanks baby"

After serving Felicia, L went back to the couch to finish counting his money. Less than ten minutes later, there was another knock at the front door. L got up and looked out the window. This time L saw a German Shepard sitting in front of the house, he automatically knew who it was at the door.

Uncle Sam was L's runner, and not your average smoker. Back in the days Uncle Sam was getting the most money on the block. L and Uncle Sam have been getting money together ever since L first started hustling. It was Uncle Sam that first caught L hustling.

L was fourteen years old living in a house that was three houses from Uncle Sam's spot. Every day and night L saw crack heads running in and out Uncle Sam's crack house. One day L decided to buy a double up from this other hustler named Cat. With the double up, L started catching some of the crackheads that was going to Uncle Sam's spot to purchase from Uncle Sam.

When Uncle Sam found out that L was serving some of his customers, he didn't get mad at the youngster, he was honestly impressed to see a young dude trying to get some money and wasn't in the street wildling out. Uncle Sam confronted L and offered him a proposition, he told L that it was alright for him to serve his customers just as long as he copped his product from him. From that day, L been hustling and selling crack. L learned the game from Uncle Sam, and his mother Lisa.

When Uncle Sam started getting high, L really stepped his game up. L began investing into property. L owned several houses in his hood and rented one of them to one of Uncle Sam's Ladies. She had section eight which was guaranteed money rent money for L, and there was also a bonus with the house for L.

Uncle Sam would turn the house into a smoke house. All the crack heads could turn their tricks there and get high as long as they copped their work from Uncle Sam. Uncle Sam would then run all of the money to L, and L would hit Uncle Sam properly to a point that Uncle Sam would be able to make something extra for him-self. Not only was

L getting section eight money for a tore up house that he was renting, but he was also making a killing off that same house with hustling.

Uncle Sam had a smooth pimp swag and was the best that L saw train a dog. When L was sixteen years old, he would post up on the block with his comrades, Uncle Sam would walk up with his dog and bet a hundred dollars that if L and his comrades had any drugs stashed in the vicinity, his dog could find it.

Every time they made that bet, Uncle Sam would win. There were times that Uncle Sam would come down the street with his dog and would tell his dog to sit and stay. Uncle Sam would then hop in a car with somebody, leave, come back and the dog would still be right there in that same spot sitting and waiting for him to come back. Whenever you saw Uncle Sam, you would also see his dog too. Some other smokers told L that when Uncle Sam was messed up in the game, he would go to the

West Side and have his dog sniff out other drug dealer stashes to get back on.

For the last two days Uncle Sam been running L all the money. Since L was down to his last three bricks, he decided to bust them down and only sell weight to his comrades from his block. When L noticed that it was Uncle Sam at the front door, he opened the door to let him inside the house. Before Uncle Sam entered the house, he turned around and looked at his dog.

"Don't move until I get back"

Uncle Sam turned around and walked in the house closing the door behind him.

"I'm feeling your energy nephew, you staying down like a true hustler."

Uncle Sam was also game tight and knew how to talk up on a hand-out, but L was all too familiar with Uncle Sam's ways.

"Cut da bullshit out Unc, and let's just get down to business".

L walked past Uncle Sam going back into the living room.

"Yeah let's get down to business because da way you talking it sound like you tired of getting dis money."

Uncle Sam said in a sarcastic tone. L stood near the couch looking at Uncle Sam.

"Nigga I've been up for damn near three days straight."

"Well get used to it Nephew, because around here we don't sleep, we just take cat naps."

L couldn't help but laugh at Uncle Sam's slick remark. Uncle Sam then went inside of his pocket and pulled out some money, he licked his fingertips and started counting the money.

"Here nephew, dis a hundred and twenty dollars."

Uncle Sam passed L the money.

L took the money and counted it again to make sure that it was a hundred and twenty dollars, then he walked over to the glass table in the dining room and put some crack on the scale. Once the scale read four grams, L put the crack into an empty sandwich bag and tied it up. L then walked back over to the couch where Uncle Sam was sitting at.

L tossed the bag to Uncle Sam.

"Dis four grams, now you owe me fifty dollars."

Uncle Sam began inspecting the bag and smiled at L.

"Now dats my muthafuckin Nephew."

Uncle Sam was so happy that L looked out for him, he left L with a jew.

"I swear nephew, since the first time I saw you serving one of my customers, I knew dat you were going to get out here in these streets and get you a bank roll, outta all dem young niggaz dat was ya age, you were da only one dat was really trying to get you some money, and I knew from back then dat you were a hustler. Ya see, it's a big difference between niggaz dat hustle and niggaz dat grind. A grinder knows how to make something outta nothing and grind hard to get a couple of dollars, then when he reaches a certain amount, he'll fall back, but a hustler though? knows only hustling because his whole life is based on hustling! He never falls back and takes a break, keep getting dat muthafuckin money Nephew, don't be like these other niggaz dat flip a few ounces and fall thinking dat they Big Meech, stay hungry and stick to the hustler script."

Although Uncle Sam had a lot of game with him, L always listened whenever he talked because he always said some real things. Uncle Sam looked at L.

"Let dat soak in, and I'm gon holla back at you, stay up."

"Aight Unc,"

After Uncle Sam left, L laid down on the couch to catch a quick cat nap. A half an hour later, L was woken up by his phone constantly going off, L answered it when he saw that the caller was Chew.

"Yo"

"Respect to the Gangsta, fuck is up? Sound like you were sleeping nigga"

While scratching his head L said

"I had to try and sneak me in a lil cat nap"

"I'm at the castle, pull up a.s.a.p. and bring a dutch"

"Aight! I'll be swinging through there in a minute"

"Bring a dutch too"

"Aight"

After ending the call with Chew, L stood up and stretched his arms out and yawned, then he hopped in the shower, and took him a nice hot and steamy shower. Once he got out the shower, he threw on his Robin Jeans, Robin T-shirt, his big Cuban link gold chain, a blue New York Yankee fitted cap with some new crispy construction Timberland boots.

It didn't matter what time of the day it was, whenever somebody rode down Dodge Street, it was always live with groups of people scattered all around. In the street it was a big crowded dice game. L pulled up to the dice game in his Lexus LS 500 and rolled his window down.

"What da bank looking like?"

L's little man Jay Jay was shaking up the dice, and looked to his other hand that was filled with money

"I don't know, it's about three stacks in here."

L smiled at Jay Jay.

"I'll be back to take dat shit!"

"You could pull over now and get some."

Jay Jay went in his left pocket and pulled out another bank roll. "Because it's more where dat came from."

Another young dude named Ant waved his bank roll to L.

"You not da only nigga getting money."

L laughed as he pulled off. When he got to the corner, it was another group of dudes posted up. L rolled down his passenger window.

"Wut up?"

Hav started walking up to L's Lexus.

"I was just about to call you. I need some work."

"What you tryna get?"

L asked while leaning back in his seat. Hav leaned his head into the window.

"At least a brick"

"I might not have a brick, I gotta check"

"It's dry out here, I'm down to my last ounces"

"Give me a minute, I'm a try and put something together for you"

"Please do, word up!"

Hav stepped back from the car. L looked at Hav.

"I'll be back."

L placed the gear in drive.

"Yup."

While L pulled off, he beeped the horn at the crowd posted up at the store. The crowd waved back. Once L came to the stop sign, he turned his music up and murked off real fast leaving skid marks in the street. L had a thing for racing cars and was nice behind the steering wheel. L was also known for taking the cops on high speed chases and getting away. While he was speeding to Chew's house, he was listening to Yo Gotti and rapping the lyrics to the song.

"I'm a die a real Nigga, I'm a die a real Nigga,

I ain't soft on these hoes, I ain't crossing on

my folk, feds come and scoop me, my mouth

staying closed, cause I'm a die a real nigga."

Chew and L have been best friends since they were little kids. The bond they shared was more of a brotherly bond. They were alike in some ways but different in most. Chew was five foot nine inches weighing two hundred and twenty pounds. Chew was solid and had a nice size. Even with the waves spinning in his hair, most people say he look like the rapper Young Jeezy. Chew was originally from Cold Spring, a section on the Eastside of Buffalo, NY.

When Chew was a teenager, his mom bought a house uptown. Every weekend Chew would spend the night at L house in Coldspring. Chew was a good kid up until his father, Flash, fell victim to crack. Flash was the nicest basketball player in Buffalo, he had a scholarship to Buffalo State College and was recruited to the NBA.

But Flash would mess all of that up by getting hooked on to crack cocaine. Before Flash fell victim, life was good for Chew and his family and Chew enjoyed every bit of it. Chew really wanted his father to make it to the NBA. It hurt Chew when his father messed up his hoop dreams from crack.

When the crack started taking its toll on Flash causing problems in the family, Chew's mother Janice threatened Flash. Janice told Flash if he didn't get his shit together, her and Chew were leaving. Flash checked into a rehab and have been clean ever since.

One day while Janice was driving home from visiting Flash in the rehab, she was involved in a deadly car accident. Chew was hurt from losing his mother and blamed crack for destroying his family. He made a promise to his self that he would never sell crack or any other drugs that could destroy you and break up families.

Chew started robbing drug dealers and became a killer after losing his mother. Flash took Janice's death hard too. When he was released from the rehab, he never did any drugs again. After her death, Flash and

Chew's bond grew stronger. Flash became Chew's handyman and took care of all his legitimate business. Truth be told, Chew was still angry that crack messed up his family and caused his father his NBA career. Whenever Chew robbed a drug dealer, he didn't have one bit of remorse in him, he treated the robbery game as if it was his job.

Other than robbing drug dealers, Chew had other source of income. Chew had a weed house on the West Side of Buffalo that was doing crack money numbers, he also had a vending machine business. Chew had about twenty machines in factories break rooms filled with soda's and snacks and was making a nice penny off them, he had a service van that provided transportation to families in New York State that had a family member or a loved one locked up in the Department of Corrections.

Chew let his father run all the legit businesses while he focused on the dirty money. Chew was very smart and a low-key type of guy with a serious demeanor. He wasn't the loud and flashy type of guy, he didn't smoke weed, gamble or wear chains. He was a killer that played the background and spent most of his midnights plotting on heavy weight drug dealers. He didn't really like to be outside during the day. Chew was more about the night life type a guy.

L, on the other hand was the life of the party, he was born and raised on Dodge Street, better known as Dodge Town. Another hood in Coldspring. Due to a lot of inside hood beef, Dodge Town never really considered themselves Coldspring, although they were in the same hood. L always lived around Dodge Town, he never lived anywhere else. He was strictly Dodge Town.

L was six feet three inches and weighed two hundred and fifteen pounds. L had long braids and was often told that he favored the NBA Basketball player Carmelo Anthony. Unlike Chew, L never knew his father and didn't care to know about him. L's mother, Lisa, raised him all by herself in Coldspring. Lisa was one of the baddest females in Coldspring, she was all about her bread and was one of the best boosters in the town. Lisa kept L and Chew in the latest fashion.

Instead of a Mother and Son bond, Lisa and L had more of a big sister and little brother bond. When Lisa caught L selling crack at the age of fourteen, she didn't flip out on him. Instead Lisa decided to school L on the game and teach him how to stack his money, and invest into Real Estate. L was lucky enough to have been taught the game from both, his Mother and Uncle Sam.

L was heavy in the crack game but was smart enough to know he would need other sources of income. Other than selling crack, L's legitimate source of income was his rental properties. L owned several houses around Dodge Town, and five more on the West Side. Chew's weed house was one of L's houses. Flash did all the maintenance on all of L's houses. L was real flashy and a lady's type of guy.

Instead of robbing drug dealers like Chew, L was in the drug game. Chew was born on Northampton Street, which is a street in Cold Springs. But was raised on Goodyear Ave. Although he moved to Goodyear Ave, he would still make his way back home to the Cold Springs. L was born and raised on Dodge Street.

Northampton Ave and Dodge Street were just a block apart from each other. Ever since the second grade the boys were friends and now with L being twenty-seven years old and Chew being a year younger, they were more like brothers. They had a lot of opposites, but they also had some things in common. Other than then getting money, their gun game was something else they had in common. They both were killers, with multiple bodies under their belts.

*** Chapter 2 ***

Chew lived in a nice house in West Seneca, which was a nice area located outside of South Buffalo. L was speeding so fast, it only took him fifteen minutes to get to Chew house. While L was putting his key in Chew's front door, a strong skunk smell smacked him right in the face.

When L walked in Chew's house, Flash and Chew were at the dining room table with the table full of weed. Flash was holding a big folder with some paperwork and pictures in his hands, Chew was putting the weed into small jars. The table had at least a thousand-dollar worth of small jars on it. L walked into the dining room, and looked at Flash.

"Pops what's up?"

"Just another day Son. How you been?"

"You know me, just taking it one day at a time"

L sat down at the dining room table. Flash looked at L.

"I hear dat."

Chew tossed over one of those small jars that was filled with weed to L.

"Here bro. Roll dat up and let me know what I'm working with."

L examined the weed.

"Shit from the looks of it and from the way it smells I can tell you right now it's some fire, you need to light some insects, you could smell this shit from the front porch. Word up!"

L caught the jar with his left hand. Chew looked at L.

"Don't even worry because dis shit about to be up outta here real soon."

Chew started stuffing more jars with weed. While L was gutting the Dutch Master, Flash opened the folder and showed L some pictures. "Check out this laundry mat dis guy got for sale over there in the University Plaza."

"Dat's a good business to invest in."

Flash looked at L.

"Maybe you should partner up with Chew and get it."

L pulled out his Bic lighter from his left pocket, lit the Dutch and inhaled.

"Dats not my league Pops, I don't have patience for dat. Dat's more of Chew style."

Chew laughed and looked at Flash.

"Pops you know dat L is not really into dis legit money."

Shaking his head, Flash was still looking at L.

"Trust me, this a great location to have a laundry mat."

L looked at Flash.

"I wonder why da owner is selling it."

Chew looked at L.

"Because da blacks is now moving around there, you already know dat you can't put too many of us around each other without shit popping off."

L pointed his left finger at Chew.

"Dat's exactly my point! I been done killed me one of them lil niggaz up there. I don't have da patience for dat!"

Chew and Flash both laughed out loud because they knew that L was serious.

"I'm a just stick to da game and my houses,"

Flash looked at the time on his phone, then stood up.

"Well I gotta go, I have a couple of meetings."

Chew started heading towards the back door.

"Okay. Pops try and lock those deals in for da laundry mat and dat charter bus, and pull ya truck up to the back door, so da neighbors don't see you taking those duffle bags out."

"Don't worry son, I'm going to work my magic."

Flash walked towards the front door. Chew looked at Flash.

"And tell Snoop I'll be pulling up in a minute."

"Aight Son, y'all be safe."

After Flash walked out the door, Chew told L to help Flash with putting the three duffle bags in his pick-up truck.

L finished helping Flash and went back in the house and noticed another duffel bag by the dining room table.

"Pops forgot another duffel bag."

Chew looked at L.

"Naw, dat bag for you."

Chew stood up brushing the weed off his lap. L look at the bag with a shocked facial expression.

"Let me find out you stung another lic?"

L opened the duffel bag and couldn't believe his eyes.

"Bro it gotta be over ten bricks in dis bag"

Chew smiled at L.

"Nigga it's twenty-five of dem thangs in there, fuck is you talking about? We back nigga!"

L looked at Chew and smiled.

"You da coldest bro, hands down nigga you da coldest I've seen hit lics."

L gave Chew some daps and a brotherly love hug. Chew looked at L.

"I told you Bro, just let me play my position, and I'm gon get us back! Nigga this what I do!"

Chew smiled at L. L had to sit down and spark up his blunt and soak up everything.

"Ayo bro, dis not no average nigga dat you stung, you just hit a nigga dats connected, put me on to who you just hit because this some real shit, word up!"

Chew was never the type a guy to brag or talk about who he robbed, but L was his bro, so he didn't mind telling him.

"You know da old school nigga Jac dat be pushing dat new all black Navigator?"

L inhaled his blunt trying to place a face on da old school guy named Jac.

"Yeah I know exactly who you talking about, I heard dat he be hitting mad niggaz with work in da town, a lot of niggaz is supposedly eating off his plate."

"Well I've been studying da nigga for damn near da last six months and when da time was right, I struck."

With a serious facial expression, L looked at Chew.

"Keep it a buck bro, how much you hit em for?"

"See, now nigga you getting a little too nosey."

Chew started laughing.

"Nigga who sent you? But naw, I hit dat nigga for fifty of them thangs and fifty pounds, something light na mean."

L had the same shock facial expression on his face from before.

"Get da fuck outta here?"

"Man, dat shit was like taking candy from a baby, word up."

"Then where da the other bricks at?"

"Don't worry about dat, just know dat I got dem joints for you at twenty a brick"

"Shit, I'm going to cop dat from you ASAP, as a matter of fact, I want five of dem thangs right now."

Chew nod his head agreeing with L.

"I got you"

L looked at Chew with a serious facial expression.

"But on some G shit, did you take care of him? Because you know dat you can't leave niggas like him alive"

"I gotta double back."

"What you mean you gotta double back?"

"When I hit his stash-house, he wasn't there but his sister was. I walked her in and tied her up. I was hoping that I could have caught him at da spot and knocked him off right then and there, but instead of him coming to da house his sister came, and I couldn't let dat opportunity pass by. I had to handle my business, but I got da nigga mapped out. I know all his where about. Once I get everything situated, I'm doubling back and knocking him off"

"Yeah we gotta knock this nigga off A.S.A.P. because it's only a matter of time that he'll find out dat it was you"

L leaned back in the chair. Chew looked at L.

"Nigga I was masked up'

"I know but trust me, niggaz like him with long money could easily put a puzzle together and find out, he was feeding a lot of niggaz, he could have shooters from all over hitting at us, just hurry up and get situated, and we gon knock this nigga off"

"I know da spots dat he be playing. From where he eats at, to where he rests his head at. I just gotta get a few things in order and

I'm gon track him down. I don't even need you to ride with me on this one."

Chew winked his eye at L, and started walking towards his room.

"Naw, I'm with you on this one!"

Chew looked at L.

"Ayo, put dat smoke on da table in dat empty duffel bag, let me change real fast, we gotta make a few stops."

Chew disappeared into the room.

"Aight."

L started grabbing the bag. When Chew returned to the dining-room, he had on an all-black and white striped Adidas tracksuit, with the all-white stripped shell toed matching Adidas shoes, a black New York Yankee fitted cap, and his Rolex watch with his big pinky ring. Chew threw his Cadillac Escalade truck keys over to L and grabbed two duffel bags.

"Come on Bro you drive"

When L got on the expressway, Chew turned the music up. They rode in deep thoughts listening to the Meek Millz song that was blasting through the speakers:

"My trigger finger itching, palms itching too. We back-to-back in ghosts playing peek-a-boo. We went to war with Sosa over a break or two. So, for 100 keys think what my clique a do. I'm talkin clappin toasts, bullets a hit ya roof"

Their first stop was Uptown so Chew could serve some of the dudes over there some pounds of weed, then the next stop was over to Chew weed house on the West side.

While they were coming off the Expressway approaching a red traffic light, Chew noticed an all-white on white 750 Beamer cruising through the intersection.

"Ayo, who dat driving dat white beamer?"

L looked at Chew.

"Remember da Twins from North Buffalo? Keyshawn and Tyeshawn?"

Chew looked at L.

"Yeah you talking about da ballplayers?"

L nod his head agreeing with Chew.

"Yeah, dat's Tyeshawn joint. I heard dem boys playing in dat dope game, he getting a couple of dollars. Tyeshawn been out here tryna make a name for himself, they talking about he been out here putting his gun game down too"

L pulled off from the light. Chew looked at L with one of his eye brows raised and a smile on his face like something was funny.

"Dat nigga Tyeshawn putting his gun game down out here?"

L laughed out loud.

"Dat's what they're saying!"

Chew shook his head as if he couldn't believe what he was hearing.

"Dat's crazy, you know da game is fucked up out here when you got sweet niggaz like him running around fronting like he's really about dat life."

"I can't call it with des niggaz out here, word up."

When Chew got to two streets from his weed house, he called Snoop phone. Once Snoop answered his call, Chew only said three words, "I'm pulling up", and ended his call.

Snoop knew exactly what those three words meant. They meant to grab the 12-gauge shotgun and post-up by the door just in case if somebody was laying on Chew. L parked Chew's truck in front of Flash's garage in the back yard where Chew usually parked it. After parking the truck, the both of them gripped their guns, and grabbed the last duffel bag and walked over to the weed house.

Snoop was the youngest one from the Dodge Town, he was seventeen years old and just like Chew and L were close like brothers, him and Jay Jay were close like brothers. Snoop was like a little brother to Chew, and Chew was like the Big Brother that Snoop never had.

Growing up as a youngster, Snoop had a hard life, he never knew his father and his mother was strung out on drugs. Snoop mother, Shirley, would sell all her food stamps and spend all her money on drugs. Snoop didn't have a decent outfit or sneakers for school. Anything in their household that had any value to it, she was selling it to support her drug addiction.

Dodge Town dudes basically took care of Snoop. Shirley was so strung out on drugs and was so busy chasing her next high, she never cared about Snoop's whereabouts, if he ate or if he didn't eat. When Snoop was just nine years old, he was already off the porch and into the streets. He was a tough kid that was fearless.

As Snoop became older, Chew noticed just how deep Snoop was getting in the streets because he now started playing with guns. Chew snatched Snoop up quickly and put him under his wing. Chew opened a weed house up and let Snoop run it.

Chew took care of Snoop, treating him like a real little brother, and Snoop had mad love for Chew for doing that. Snoop was now seventeen years old and getting money and had a nice stash of money put up. Although, it was a weed house that had bars all around the windows, the house was laced up on the inside, nice furniture, flat screen TV's, and a refrigerator full of food.

Chew let Snoop live in the house under a few rules, no handguns were allowed in the house, no playing loud music, and only his one main girlfriend was able to come over. Chew knew how emotional females could be, and the last thing he wanted was for his weed house to get raided all because a female got jealous about Snoop having another girl in the house with him.

Snoop didn't mind following the rules, most of the time he had his main girlfriend

Tiara spending the night with him. Tiara was nineteen years old and was in love with Snoop. She cooked good meals for Snoop and kept the house clean. She was the only girl that could control Snoop. Tiara wasn't scared of Snoop or going for none of his player ways.

Snoop was standing in the doorway with a 12-gauge shotgun in his hand while Chew and L was coming up the stairs with their guns in their hands. L looked at Snoop.

"What's up lil nigga?"

Snoop looked at L and Chew.

"Respect to the Gangtaz"

Chew and L smiled back at Snoop and they both responded back saying, "Respect."

While Chew was walking through the living-room he noticed Tiara laying on the couch watching a DVD.

"What's up young lady?"

Tierra looked at Chew.

"Hey Bro,"

"I see you in here watching dat Paid In Full."

Tiara shook her head.

"Dats Snoop watching this shit, he watches it at least twenty times a day"

Tiara looked at Snoop and rolled her eyes. Snoop was walking towards the kitchen shaking his head.

"Don't nobody be saying nothing when you be going on Demand watching da same episodes of Love and Hip Hop at least fifty times a day."

"And you be in here watching it right with me! Don't be in here tryna to front for ya peoples!"

Tiara laughed out loud. While following Snoop to the kitchen L and Chew was laughing at Tiara respond. Snoop looked at L and Chew

"Dat broad is crazy, yo, word up!"

Chew walked over to the kitchen table and put the duffel bag on it and opened it. Chew began taking the weed out the duffel bag, and Snoop opened a Nike sneaker box that was filled with money. Snoop looked at Chew.

"It's been bleeding, they've been coming to da window nonstop."

L looked at Snoop.

"Dat's what's up, get dat money. Lil Nigga!"

Snoop smiled at L.

"You know dat shit!"

Chew looked at Snoop, and slid him a few zip-lock bags full of jars.

"Dis should hold you down for minute"

"Aight!"

While zipping up the duffle bag, Chew looked at Snoop.

"You and your girl hungry?"

"Naw we good, Pops came through and brought us some KFC."

Snoop followed Chew and L to the door. Chew turned around at the door.

"Aight hit me up if you need me, I gotta take care of some business."

Chew looked at L and said,

"Come on Bro, I gotta go and check out da laundromat."

L gave Snoop some daps and a brotherly hug.

"Aight Lil Nigga, hold it down."

"Always."

The University Plaza was located close to a college campus, it was so close you would have thought the university Plaza was on the college campus. Most of the University Plaza customers were college students. The plaza was made up of several stores. Other than Tops grocery store the Plaza was now black owned.

It had a popular record store, a good soulful restaurant, a popular nail shop, and the laundry mat. When L pulled into the

Plaza it was busy as usual. It didn't take long for Chew to notice his father's grey Ford F-150 pickup truck parked right in front of the laundry mat. Chew looked at L.

"Bro, pull up next to Pop's truck."

When L parked the truck next to Flash's pickup truck, Chew noticed flash was inside the laundry mat talking to the owner, he decided to stay outside until his father was done talking business with the owner.

While Chew and L sat in the truck with the AC on, they observed the Plaza. The laundromat was right next to a black owned nail shop. The nail shop had a lot of females going in and out regularly. A few people stopped at the laundry mat as they were walking by an asked if the laundry mat was going to open back up. L noticed a familiar face from one of the ladies that was in the nail shop. L looked at Chew.

"Ayo Bro, you see da thick brown skinned shorty with da pink Jays on her feet?"

"Yeah!"

"She da owner of dat nail shop and her mother own a few of these spots. They own dat record store, and da soul food restaurant."

Chew looked at L.

"And let me guess, you smashed dat?"

L laughed out loud.

"Naw, shorty don't be tryna give a nigga no play. I never blast at her, niggaz be saying dat shorty don't be out there like dat, you know who her father is right?"

Chew shrugged his shoulders.

"Naw, who her father?"

L looked at Chew like he was crazy.

"Nigga, Gator is her father!"

"Gator?"

Chew repeated the name as if he was trying to place a face on the name Gator.

"Who da fuck is Gator?

"Da nigga Gator dat had da town on smash back in da days."

Chew nod his head.

"Oh, dat Gator, didn't they put dat nigga lights out?"

"I heard they gave dat nigga twenty-five to life."

"Dat's a mean pill to swallow."

"Word up, but you know how dis shit go when you playing this game"

Gator was an official kingpin that had majority of Buffalo on lockdown. He had a lot of dudes from his generation under pressure. Although Gator was in the feds serving a life sentence, he still had his hand in the dope game in Buffalo, he was still getting money and had a few legit shops in the University Plaza that he let his daughter Precious and wife Darlene run for him.

L nod his head towards the stores in the Plaza.

"If I'm not mistaken, he da one dat own those three spots over there, they say dat niggaa money is longer than train smoke, from da feds, he still eating off these streets, he must be tryna clean his money through these spots in this Plaza."

Chew looked at L with a serious facial expression.

"How much you think dat nigga worth?"

L laughed out loud.

"Look at you!"

Chew laughed out loud too.

"You a funny nigga"

Chew looked at L.

"On some G shit tho, I wouldn't get at him when it's so many other lics out here. I respect da fact dat he locked up still tryna feed his family, but if I ever get fucked up out here, and there's nobody else on the menu, I'll get dat nigga. I don't give a fuck about how many bodies he got, or how strong his team is out here. I don't give a fuck about none of dat shit, word up! It's a new era out here, these niggaz bleed just like us, but for da most part, I'm good! My money is up. I'll just keep hitting these other clowns out here."

Chew smiled at L.

"Na mean"

L laughed out loud.

"You a wild boy, word up you a wild nigga! Come on bro let's walk down here to this soulful restaurant and get us something to eat, I'm hungry as hell."

Chew opened the door to his truck and followed behind L. They hopped out the truck looking like new money to the thirsty females that was standing outside the nail shop being nosy. All eyes were on them as they walked pass the nail shop.

Precious was at the door of her nail shop and instead of being thirsty, checking Chew and L out, she just gave them a regular look and went back into her shop.

Chew got the impression that Precious was one of them spoiled girls that thought she was all that because of her good looks and father's reputation. Females with an attitude like the impression Precious were giving to Chew, he didn't like to talk to.

It was obvious that the females were checking them out. Chew looked at L with a serious facial expression.

"I'm telling you now bro, if I get this laundry mat spot, don't be fucking these thirsty bitches and having them all up at my spot looking for you and showing out! We not going to have dat up at my place of business."

"Nigga you bugging out!"

L said looking at Chew.

"I'm not thinking about these hoes. I'm thinking about dis muthafuckin money word up! I'm about to bleed da hood and have it leaking"

When they walked into the soul food restaurant it was a pretty, sexy, older lady that had to be in her late fifties working and taking orders. The lady looked like an older version of Precious. Chew could tell that the lady had to be Precious mother.

"Hello, how you fellas doing?"

The lady asked them from behind the counter. Chew looked at the older lady.

"Alright and ya self?

The lady replied.

"I can't complain."

L looked at the Lady.

"You got it smelling good in here."

Chew looked at L.

"Yeah, she do got it smelling good"

The lady smiled at L and Chew.

"Well it also tastes good, what would you gentlemen like to order?"

L looked at the lady.

"I don't even need a menu. I'll take a chicken dinner with a loganberry"

While feeling his pockets for his phone, Chew looked at the lady.

"And I'm going to take a fish dinner with a loganberry too"

The lady wrote down the orders.

"Alright, it'll be a few minutes."

Chew and L stood by a table and held a conversation with each other while the lady took care of their order. While they were talking, Flash came into the restaurant smiling. Chew looked at his father.

"Tell me something good pops."

"We got it!"

Flash looked at the lady who just took L and Chew's order.

"Hey Darlene."

"Hey Flash, how you doing?

"I could be better, but I'm hanging in there."

Flash smiled at Darlene.

"I know dat's right."

Darlene then looked at Chew.

"This gotta be your boy, because he looks just like you. I swear y'all look like Twins."

Flash laughed out loud.

"Yeah, dat's my son"

Darlene kept her eyes on Chew.

"Boy you look just like ya father."

Darlene looked at Flash.

"I was looking at him saying to myself, he looks familiar."

Darlene looked up as if she were trying to gather up her thoughts with her right hand on her hip.

"He gotta be twenty-five because him Precious is around da same age"

Flash looked at Chew like he forgot his age.

"Chew you twenty-five, right?"

Chew shook his head.

"Pops I'm twenty-six."

"Boy you know dat I'm getting old."

Darlene looked at Chew with a smile on her face.

"Ya father was da best basketball player in Buffalo."

After twenty minutes Darlene had their food ready. L gave her thirty dollars and told her to keep the change.

While they were walking back to the laundromat, Chew looked at Flash.

"Let me find out dat you were cheating on Mama love with dat lady Pops! I could just imagine how sexy she looked back in da days because she still looking good for her age now!"

L looked at Chew and smiled.

"Yeah Pops cheated!"

Chew laughed out loud.

"Hell yeah"

L looked at Chew.

"Word up! Pops hit dat."

Flash looked at them.

"Y'all two need to stop, she was something to look at tho, but dat was Gator's thang, we all went to high school together, and me and Gator was playing ball on the same team, Darlene used to come up to our games."

While reaching for the laundry mat door, L looked at Flash.

"Pops it's alright if you hitting dat because I would a knocked her ass down too!"

Chew was still laughing.

"He know dat he was smashing dat"

Flash just shook his head and looked at Chew and L like they were crazy.

*** Chapter 3 ***

Every hood in Buffalo had their own hustlers, killers, stick up kids, cons and players. Each hood mainly had one thing they were known for. Cold Springs had their fair share of hustlers, each hood in Cold Springs had a few heavyweight hustlers, but what they really were known for was their gun game. Cold Springs bred stone cold killers.

Inside of Cold Springs there were nine sections, and each section had a nice size of territory. A lot of the hustlers in Cold Springs were switching their hustle over to the dope game. The dope game was slowly taking over, but at the same time, it was still hustlers dealing with the crack game.

Usually the heavy weight hustlers in Cold Springs would plug from each other whenever one of them had a good connect. Cold Springs dudes didn't too much deal with other dudes from outside of the hood. One of them would take a trip down South and get some bricks for a low price and come back to the hood and would sell to each other for a decent price. Although they were taking all the risks by transporting it back to Buffalo, they still sold the bricks to each other for a decent price out of hood respect.

L knew how to cook up his own work, but Uncle Sam knew a few tricks to the trade to cooking. L decided to let Uncle Sam cook up some of his work in the kitchen while L and five of his main hitters from Dodge Town watched him.

Once Uncle Sam cooked up the first brick, L gave him a nice size and told him to go in the bathroom and test it out. About three minutes later Uncle Sam came out the bathroom looking zoned out.

L looked at him. "So, what I'm working with?"

"You could throw a quarter of dat thang on each brick and still come young B plus."

L did the math in his head real quick, he could get five bricks off four bricks. Each brick would be a brick and a quarter brick. L looked around at his comrades.

"Now, dats plenty of room for boys to be able to bless these smokers and still eat good." L said catching eye contact with all of them.

All of his comrades were his day one, dudes dat he knew his whole life. They were official and from Dodge Town just like him and Chew was. Most of them were already playing with a brick or two in their game and was seeing good profits from busting their bricks down.

Hav, Jimmy, Kaboom, and Nut was just a little younger than L, but they all were a beast in the game. They were all about getting money and that gunplay life. E and Kaboom was more of hustlers than shooters, but if push came to shove those two would pick up their guns and put that work in.

Hav looked at E.

"Yeah we could corner the market and just bust our bricks down."

"Exactly! And if we bless our smoker word is gon get around and it's gon attract more smokers."

Jimmy looked at everybody.

"Shitd, I'm all in!"

L looked at everybody.

"Aight cool, this what we gon do, I'm gon toss y'all out a quarter thang to get started don't worry about selling weight, just focus on blessing our smokers. Instead of bagging up we going with da dump truck game and hit the smokers for anything from three dollars and up. As far as da weight lics goes? leave it up to me!"

Nut looked at L.

"Aight! What about dem lil niggaz"

Kaboom nod his head agreeing with Nut.

"Word, because dem lil niggaz be wildling, spitting on fiends and shit."

L looked at them.

"Don't worry about dem lil niggaz, I'm gon make sure dat they straight too"

L looked at his phone for the time.

"They should be pulling up any minute. Oh yeah and another thing, it's a wrap for all dat inside Cold Springs beefing shit. I'm about to form an alliance with niggaz. It's time for niggaz to put dat shit to da side and come together on some real get money shit"

Hav shook his head.

"Good luck with dat shit, niggaz egos is too big to come together, if it wasn't for certain niggaz plugging from each other, dis shit would be a jungle out here for real."

E looked at Hav.

"Dat's a fact!"

L looked them.

"Just let me handle it!"

As soon as L finished his sentence, there was a knock at the front door, L motioned his head to Kaboom for him to answer the door.

Kaboom went to the door.

"It's Jay Jay and dem."

L looked at Kaboom.

"Let dem in."

When they came into the house, Jay Jay smiled at L.

"Respect to the gangsta."

"Respect."

Everybody that was already in the house gave Jay Jay and the other dudes that was with him some daps and a brotherly love hug. From the fitted jeans and T-shirt that he was wearing you could see Jay Jay gun sticking out.

Before heading out the door, Hav looked back at L.

"Ayo, we bout to hit da block and get dis shit popping."

"Aight hit me up if you need some more work."

"Yup!"

After his five-henchman left out the house, L smiled at Jay Jay and the rest of them. While walking in the kitchen to get something to drink, L looked at Jay Jay.

"Fuck is up with yall lil niggaz?"

"You tell me, shitd you do one dat called da meeting."

Jay Jay was already working with a big eighth and was known for copping nothing less than that. Sometimes he would cop a quarter brick, but a big eighth was his usual. If he didn't gamble so much, he could really step his game up. Jay Jay was young and wild, but he was L lil man. L really wanted Jay Jay to step his game up.

"Y'all lil niggaz been a little too content with just copping a big here and there, and yall been fucking up. I'm gon give y'all this one shot to catch dis wave, we about to have da hood jumping. If y'all lil niggaz is serious about getting this paper, then all y'all gotta do is stick to da script and just bear down. All dat wildling on da fiends shit is dead, word up."

L pulled out a half a brick.

"Dis a half of thang, split this shit up and break it down, no more bagging it up. From now on we're going with da dump truck game. Anything from three dollars on up we're dumping it. Don't be petty because I'm giving y'all a startup kit, show da fiends a lil love so they could spread da word dat da block got it good."

All of them was happy that L was tossing them out a quarter brick. Jay Jay looked at L.

"I hear you big bro word up, good looking"

"I'm serious about Dat wildling on da fiend shit, word up! Yall niggaz gotta stop Dat shit and just focus on getting this money. Oh yeah, and another thing, it's a rap for dat inside Coldspring beef, all dat beefing shit is over. After this half a brick is gone, it's no more lookouts so make sure y'all make dis work".

Jay Jay looked at L.

"Don't worry bro I got it from here."

"Hav gone school y'all to da program."

"Say no more!"

After Jay Jay and them left the house, L figured that now would be a good time to see if Uncle Sam had some information about the old school cat Jac. Jac and Uncle Sam was from the same era it was a possibility that Uncle Sam knew Jac.

While sitting down in a recliner chair, L looked at Uncle Sam.

"Ayo, you know the old school cat named Jac that be pushing dat new all black Navi?"

"Yeah I know Jac, he been out here getting it for a long time, he had a nice run out here in these streets, Jac money is long for real."

Uncle Sam lit up a cigarette. L looked at Uncle Sam.

"What's up with him?"

L asked boldly.

"Jack is from the old school, shitd truth be told, he da reason why all dem South Buffalo niggaz is eating, Jac been playing with bricks since da eighties, why you asking about Jac?"

L had to throw a curveball in at Uncle Sam so he wouldn't catch on to him trying to pick him for information about Jac.

"Nah I was just asking because these niggaz out here be talking about him like he was up there with Gator."

"Don't get me wrong, Gator was dat nigga! But Gator and Jac were two different type a breed. They didn't really get along with each other. I think Gator was a little jealous of Jac because Jac was getting to dat money for real. Everybody loved Jac and Gator knew dat he couldn't really get at him because not only was Jac money super long, but because he had niggaz dat will go for him without him even giving the word. Shitd even Gator knew dat he couldn't touch Jac.

Uncle Sam paused for a minute to clear his throat.

"See, you gotta understand da difference between love and fear. Niggaz feared Gator but loved Jac. Jac wasn't the spotlight type a guy, he kept his smooth and lowkey, which is why he still out here, Gator was on some gangster shit and you see where dat land him, don't believe dat shit these niggaz be talking, niggaz tried to say dat Gator was pushing up on Jac but dat's bullshit, Gator money and power wasn't long and strong enough to push up on Jac, dat nigga Jac could have hitters from all over coming at Gator because he fed a lot of niggaz and when you feeding niggaz like how Jac is feeding niggaz, ain't nobody gonna let something happen to you, you don't even gotta push a button, niggaz gonna ride for you regardless."

L nod his head agreeing with Uncle Sam.

"It makes sense."

"You know I'm gon keep it real with you but like I said, Gator was dat nigga too, he was getting dat money, pushing up on niggaz and knocking shit down out here, but I don't think dat he could have pulled dat off on Jac, that's why he never liked Jac."

L felt like he heard enough about Jac. He now realized that Jac could be a problem. L knew that him and Chew had no other choice but to knock him off. L switched subjects with Uncle Sam and walked over to the TV stand to grab a cleaner ticket and then gave it to Uncle Sam along with his car keys and some money.

"Run down to the cleaners for me, I need you to pick up my clothes."

Uncle Sam looked at the car keys, ticket and money that L had in his hand like L was crazy.

"Fuck I look like to you? Nigga my name ain't no Muthafuckin Jeffery da Butler and you ain't da Fresh Prince around this bitch."

L burst out laughing.

"For real unc, I need you to handle dat for me"

"Nigga, you got this shit all da way twisted, we not about to make this a habit."

L shook his head.

"Yeah, yeah, I appreciate you."

While Uncle Sam walked out the door, he yelled,

"Shit, I bet you do!"

After Uncle Sam came back with L's clothes from the cleaners, L got dressed. L threw on his purple Ralph Lauren polo shirt, some blue jeans, new crispy all-white up towns, his big Cuban link gold chain, and an all blue New York Yankee fitted cap. Since he had two hours to spare L decided to go and get a car wash at Johnny Car Wash.

Johnny Car Wash was a popular car wash spot in Buffalo. All the dope boys and sexy ladies went there. The car wash was so big and had so many workers that it could wash and clean three cars at once.

L was leaning back in his Lexus smoking a blunt with the music blasting when he pulled up to the car wash. All eyes were on L when he pulled into the car wash. L stepped out his Lexus and was followed by a big cloud of smoke. All the workers were happy to see L because they knew that he would leave behind a good tip if they washed and detailed his car good.

While L was walking to the waiting area, he noticed the all-white on white 750 beamer the twin from North Buffalo be driving in front of his car getting detailed. Sitting next to twin was a sexy dark skin female that could give the rapper Nicki Minaj a run for her money in sex appeal.

When it came to pretty and sexy ladies, L had his fair share of them going crazy over him. His swag demanded attention. While L was sitting down in the waiting area, he kept glancing at the sexy female sitting next to the twin Tyeshawn. L already knew Tyeshawn, and Tyeshawn knew about L. Although, Tyeshawn was getting money now and was making a name for himself, he didn't wanna chance his luck with L.

Deep down inside L felt like Tyeshawn was soft and L was the type of dude that would expose you quick. While Tyeshawn was sitting next to the sexy lady, L noticed they wasn't talking to each other. It wasn't hard to figure out they were on bad terms or just wasn't feeling each other. When L finally locked eyes with the sexy female he smiled and winked his eye at her.

The female smiled back and shook her head. Tyeshawn just so happen to catch the female smiling and was wondering what it was that had her smiling. He looked around the waiting area to see what could be causing her to smile.

When he saw L sitting a few chairs down smiling, he figured that L was the reason why she was smiling. L was hoping that Tyeshawn would let his ego make him try and play tough, so he could handle Tyeshawn right there in front of the sexy lady, but Tyeshawn knew better. Instead of saying something to L, Tyeshawn started to wild out on the sexy lady.

"Bitch, I know dat you not sitting right here next to me tryna play me"

The sexy lady looked at Tyeshawn.

"Oh my God, what is your talking about?"

The sexy lady rolled her eyes.

"Bitch you know what I'm talking about."

Tyeshawn pointed his finger into the lady's face.

"Keep playing with me, and I'm gon smack da shit outta you."

The sexy female turned her head and put her head down with both of her hands on her head like she had a painful headache.

One of the car wash workers walked up to Tyeshawn with his car keys in hand, telling Tyeshawn that his car was done. Tyeshawn then looked at the girl.

"Get your muthafuckin ass in the car."

Tyeshawn paid the car wash worker and as he was walking to his car, he looked L straight in the eyes. L stared back with the facial expression that basically said it's whatever you want it to be. L then placed his hand on his gun that was on his hip. Tyeshawn just hopped in his car and pulled off. L laughed and said to himself "Ol sucka for love ass nigga."

****

The deal with Chew getting the laundromat was official, and Chew didn't waste no time at getting things situated. Dressed in a pair of blue Balmain denim jeans, a white Balmain short sleeve button down shirt, his Breitling watch, and new pair of construction timberland boots, Chew sat at a table with his father inside the laundry mat. Chew and Flash were looking at pictures of a Charter buses for his bus service.

"Son this is a perfect size. We could fit more passengers on this bus and make more money, I'm sure I can get the guy to sell it to us for a decent price, this is more of a professional type of bus for the business".

Chew was impressed with the charter bus and knew that it would be another good investment.

"Well see if you can get it for us ASAP then."

"I'm about to meet with the guy now and see if I can make dat happen for us."

Flash stood up.

"Aight."

Chew stood up with Flash. Flash looked at Chew.

"Give me a hand with bringing the two vending machines in here, and I'll just let you stock it up while I meet up with the dealer"

While Chew and Flash were bringing the vending machines in, people were coming in from left to right to wash their clothes. The laundromat picked up business in no time. Chew was stocking the vending machines with snacks and soda cans when Darlene and Precious came into the laundry mat with two bags full of towels and wash rags. When Darlene saw Chew, she smiled at him.

"I'm so glad that you and your father decided to open up this laundry mat y'all saving me and my daughter a trip."

Chew smiled back at Darlene, he had to admit that Darlene was one fine lady. When you look at Precious you could see a younger version of Darlene. Precious was five feet one and didn't have too much of a chest but had a nice round bubble butt, a dimple on each check on her face, hazel eyes and was very sexy. Chew looked at Darlene

"Good to see that our services can help you"

While Chew was closing the vending machine that he was filling up with snacks, L's mother, Lisa, came walking through the laundromat door with a big bag smiling catching Chew by surprise.

"Hey son."

Lisa was carrying a bag of comforters.

Chew returned the smile and walked over to help Lisa with the bag. "Hey Mama Luv."

Chew grabbed one of the bags.

"Larry told me that you just opened up this laundry mat, so I figured I'd come over and support your business by washing my comforters".

Lisa pointed to the bag for Chew to place it on the floor.

"Yeah, I just opened it up about an hour ago."

Chew looked around at everybody that was in the laundry mat.

Lisa always treated Chew like he was her own son. Ever since Chew's mother died in that car accident, Lisa has been there for Chew like a mother. Lisa looked around the laundry mat with a smile.

"This is a nice laundry mat that you got yourself."

"I'm just trying to get it together."

Chew looked out the window at Lisa's Benz truck that was parked in front of the laundry mat.

"You got any more bags out there?

"Yeah I got another bag, and some laundry detergent in my backseat."

When Chew came back in with the bag, and laundry detergent he started helping Lisa with loading up a washing machine. Darlene walked by and stopped.

"I'm sorry sweetheart, I didn't get your name".

Chew looked at Darlene. "You could call me Chew."

Darlene smiled.

"Ok Chew, you have a nice day."

"Thank you, and you have a bless one as well."

Chew smiled back while watching Darlene walk out the laundry mat.

Lisa smiled at Chew, and playfully slapped him on his arm.

"Now don't be up here mixing your business with pleasure!"

Chew laughed out loud.

"Mama Love, she is old enough to be my mother."

Chew said grabbing his arm like he was in pain.

"I'm not just talking about her. I'm talking about all the other ones that are checking you out, you gotta watch these little heffas when they know dat you have a business, all they start seeing is dollar signs."

Lisa looked at Chew with serious facial expression. Chew looked at Lisa.

"I know Ms. Goody wasn't checking me out".

Chew said with a grin on his face. Lisa looked at Chew

"Boy us ladies could be checking something out without even looking at it. I've seen the way she looked at you when you were helping me."

Lisa nod her head towards the laundry bag. Chew hung out with Lisa while she washed her comforters. The University Plaza seemed to be a nice spot that Chew didn't mind hanging out at during the daytime and that was something out of the ordinary. Chew wasn't a daytime type of guy, he was a night life type of guy.

Once Chew noticed more and more people were coming into the laundry mat, he went to his trunk and switched his regular ten shot clip to the extending 20 shot clip. With more unfamiliar faces coming around him, he started to feel naked with just ten shots on him.

Chew was sitting in the passenger seat of his truck with the door open and his feet hanging outside. Chew had his gun on his lap with an XXL magazine covering it. While Chew was sitting in the truck observing the Plaza, Precious came out of the soul food restaurant walking towards Chew with the Styrofoam food tray in her hand. When she got to the front of Chew's truck, she held the Styrofoam food tray out.

"Here, come and get your food."

Precious said with a sarcastic attitude. Chew looked at Precious with a confused facial expression shaking his head.

"I didn't order no food."

Precious put her left hand on her left hip.

"I know you didn't order no food, this a welcome meal from my mother."

"Oh thanks, but no thanks. I'm not hungry."

Chew said looking down at his phone.

Precious looked at Chew with a serious facial expression.

"Really? You gon be like dat with my mother? If I take this food back to my mother, she gon find dat real disrespectful."

The impression that Precious was giving Chew the other day was starting to come more to light. Right then and there, Chew wanted to check Precious. Chew could now tell that because of her father's reputation, Precious expected a person to let her have her way and just bow down to her. Little did Precious know, Chew didn't care about Gators reputation.

Off the strength of Darlene being respectful to Chew, he didn't want to be rude to her and turn down her food. Chew decided to accept the food and reached his hand out for Precious to bring the food to him. Chew didn't want to stand up and expose the gun he had on his lap under the magazine.

Precious rolled her eyes and didn't move.

"Oh, you really tripping now, what you think you got special delivery or something?"

With a serious facial expression, Chew looked at Precious.

"Just bring the food to me."

It was something about the way Chew raised his voice at Precious that reminded her of her father, she had to admit, her sexiness that always seemed to intimidate other guys was not working on Chew. Truth be told the fact that it was not working turned Precious on, she walked up to Chew with a fake attitude.

"I hope you don't think you got a special waitress! I'm gon let you slide with it this time."

Precious handed Chew the container of food.

Chew kept a serious facial expression on his face.

"I never placed an order for a waitress to bring me food anyway, remember or did you forget?"

Chew's demeanor was reminding Precious more of her father. It was something about him that she seen in her father not to mention that as she was walking up to him, she peeped the extended clip to his gun sticking out from the side of the XXL magazine. Precious looked at Chew.

"I can see it now me and you gon clash with dis smart ass mouth of yours."

As soon as Precious finished her sentence, L pulled into the parking space right next to the passenger side of Chew's truck real fast with the music blasting just missing Precious and Chew's passenger door by inches.

Chew quickly pulled Precious towards him with his left arm and gripped his gun with his right hand ready to start squeezing not knowing that it was L playing around.

L and Hav was in L's Lexus laughing at Precious and Chew's reaction. Precious was shaken up from L's little stunt. With a serious facial expression, Chew made eye contact with L.

"You buggin out! Come on bro you can't be doing shit like dat at my place of business, you almost got dat shit shot up playing around"

From the looks of L and Hav's eyes, Chew could tell that they were smoking and drinking. L laughed out loud.

"My bad bro, I didn't mean to scare you and ya girl!"

L was still laughing. Chew looked at L.

"Nigga, you almost got ya self smoked with dat bullshit."

Chew pointed his finger to the magazine on his lap. L kept laughing and looked at Precious.

"I didn't mean to scare you Ms. Lady."

Finally coming back to her senses, Precious tried to play it off like she wasn't scared.

"Oh, trust me, I wasn't scared for us, I was more scared for y'all, this tough guy right here wasn't about to let us go out like dat"

Precious looked back at Chew.

"Ain't dat right Chew? Cause da way you were acting with me for just bringing you some food, I know you was gon handle ya business with them for running up on us like dat right?"

Chew shook his head, he was still thinking about what just happened with L and that dumb professional driving stunt. Precious was still being sarcastic with him by referring to him as a tough guy.

The way that Chew grabbed Precious and gripped his gun when L pulled that stunt really made Precious feel secure in his arms. While Precious was walking back to her nail shop, L and Hav couldn't help but stare at her butt as it bounced with her sexy walk.

Hav was staring at Precious butt.

"Damn! Shorty got a fat ass"

Once Precious was out of ear distance, Chew got serious.

"Ayo y'all niggaz is bugging out, don't be coming up here with dat bullshit, word up!"

L and Hav hopped out L's Lexus, still smiling and laughing.

"Aight bro, it's not gon happen again."

L and Hav gave Chew some daps and a brotherly luv hug, then the three of them started talking. Hav sat on the front hood of L's car sipping on some Hennessy out of a plastic cup. L was leaning up on his driver side door while Chew was still sitting in the passenger seat of his truck with his door open and legs hanging out.

They laughed and joked around until Flash pulled up in his pickup truck. Looking at the scene and at their vehicles, people could tell they were some street dudes with money. Chew looked at Flash.

"Pops, tell me you got some good news"

Flash smiled.

"He willing to do a deal with us"

Chew smiled back at his father.

"Good!"

Flash look through the laundromat windows and noticed that it was people in there using the machines.

"I see dat it's picking up."

"Yeah, this a perfect location, I could get used to hanging out around here.

Chew looked around the plaza. L noticed the styrofoam food tray on the dashboard of Chew's truck and reached for it. Chew blocked his arm from grabbing it.

"The soul food spot is right down the plaza player."

"Dat's what's in that styrofoam?"

"Yep."

Chew put the container of food down on the driver's side of his truck. L looked at Hav.

"Come on bro, let's walk down here and get us one of these good ass dinners, since ya man wanna act funny with his shit."

Flash looked down the plaza to the soul food restaurant and saw Darlene's white Range Rover pulling off.

"I think dat y'all might just be a minute too late"

Darlene drove past them beeping the car horn and waved to them.

"Damn one of those dinners would've been just right for da kid."

Hav looked at L.

"Shitd, it's wing night at Petey Pete's tonight."

"We definitely could swing through there."

L walked up to Chew.

"What you about to get into?"

"Me and Pops gotta take care of some business, then after dat, I'm gon swing through da hood."

"Aight, if we not on da block we gon be at Pete's."

L gave Chew some dap and walked to his car.

"Yep, y'all boyz be easy."

Chew gave Hav some daps. Earlier that day after L got his car washed, he called a meeting with all of the heavyweight hustlers from each hood in Cold Spring. Bricks were going for thirty-five thousand in Buffalo, they were cheaper out of state.

Since Chew was giving L the remaining bricks at twenty thousand a brick, it left plenty of room for L to be able to sell them for a price that wasn't too far off the out-of-state price. Which would be helpful to those that took the risk of transporting bricks because they could now get them in Buffalo for a similar price. L decided to let the bricks go for thirty-two thousand a piece. This was a cheaper price than the original price for a brick and a good deal because it kept them from having to travel.

Petey Pete's lounge was a well-known bar that sits right in the heart of Cold Spring. Mainly Cold Spring dudes played at Petey Pete's. Not too many dudes from other hoods in Buffalo came to Petey Pete's, but females from all over came there. Petey Pete's was packed with sexy ladies and dudes from all over Cold Springs.

Dodge Town dudes played the back wall of the lounge. Dudes were coming from left to right copping weight from L. It didn't take much for Chew to notice that L was moving a lot of bricks. Yo Gotti song "down in the DM" was blasting through the speakers and had the dance floor jumping. Chew looked at L.

"I see you moving dem thangs in here".

"Yeah, I called a meeting with boyz and talked about getting that inside Cold Spring beef shit dead and coming together on some get money type shit. Niggaz see the bigger picture and realize how stronger we are unified, we keeping dat money in the hood. L took a sip of henny then put his arm over Chew shoulder's and leaned into him so he could hear him over the loud music. I showed love to niggaz that was fucked up in the game and from there, everybody been copping from me, bro we bout to get rich, and I got a little info about da old school cat Jac, everything situated on my behalf so whenever you ready to knock this nigga off, I'm ready".

"Dat's what's up, it's good to see dat you got ya head on ya shoulders, once pop handles everything with this charter bus for my van service, we could get dat nigga outta da way and get to this money"

While Chew and L we're talking to each other a guy name Nature that was from South Hampton Street, which is a block in Cold Spring walked up to L.

"Ayo, good looking out for that my G, dat's some fire, word up! I should be getting back at you tomorrow"

"No doubt"

Nature gave L and Chew some daps

"Aight, y'all players stay up, be safe and save some of these hoes for me".

Chew and L laughed. Hav was on the dance floor dancing with a female. Right next to where hav was dancing at, L noticed the sexy girl from the car wash that was with the twin Tyeshawn earlier dancing by herself. L told Chew that he'll be right back and walked up to the sexy girl from behind, then leaned into her and whispered in her ear

"What's up sexy?"

When the girl quickly turned around with a frown on her face, L smiled at her

"Da way ol boy was acting earlier, I'm surprised dat you was able to step out"

Once the girl realized that it was L, she smiled at him.

"I know, right? He was really tripping".

People was walking by so L reached out for the girl hand and pulled her closer to him. I don't see no ring on your finger, he act like he own you or something.

"He could be a lil possessive at times".

"Shitd, you call dat just being a lil?"

The girl couldn't help but laugh.

"So, what's ya name?"

"Trina, and your's?"

"L"

Trina looked at L.

"Did anybody ever tell you dat you look like dat basketball player Carmelo Anthony?"

"Yeah people tell me dat Melo look like me all the time"

"Oh, so he looked like you and you don't look like him?"

Trina shifted her body to her left side and fold her arms making herself look even more sexier. Right when L was about to say something to Trina, a guy from Laurel street which was another block in Cold Spring walked up to L and looked at Trina

"Pardon me sex"

The dude then leaned into L's ear. after he said something to L, L looked at him".

"Aight give me a minute and I'm gon get dat for you"

After the dude walked off, L pointed his attention back to Trina.

"So, what you doing after you leave here?"

"What's dat a trick question? Im taking my ass home".

"Fuck dat nigga, how about you get up with me I'll take care of him if he start tripping on you"

"Now, you know dat I can't do dat, but it was nice talking to you tho".

Trina was about to walk off, when L grabbed her arm.

"Well, could I at least get your number?"

"How about I'll take your's?"

After L gave Trina his number, he told her to make sure that she used it.

"I will"

When L got back to where everybody from the block was posted up at drinking and partying, he saw Chew was talking to

Shameka. She was from Buck Town which was another hood in Cold Spring.

Shameka was thick like the rapper Remy Ma and was about her money. Shemeka aslo be hustling on the block like how niggaz be hustling. Chew and Shameka wasn't in a relationship, but they've been messing around with each other for a couple of years. Shameka also used to plug pounds of weed from chew. L walked to Chew.

"Ayo bro, I gotta slide to da block and hit dis lic".

"Im bout to slide myself".

"Aight, well tell pops to take care of dat charter bus ASAP, so we could hurry up and tie up dat loose end".

"You already know dat I'm on it".

Chew gave L and everybody from Dodge Town some daps and a brotherly love hug, then him and Shameka left Petey Pete's together and hopped in his truck and headed to the house.

*** Chapter 4 ***

It didn't take long for word to spread through the streets that Dodge Town had it good. The hood was flooded with smokers from all over, everybody from Dodge Town was getting money. Jay Jay was in the middle of the street with a big crowd shooting dice. E and another group of dudes were posted up at the corner. While L and another group of dudes was posted up on Uncle Sam front porch.

The block was live as usual. While L was smoking on a blunt with his comrades, a dark blue Lincoln MKZ with smoked out dark tints rode by. Kaboom looked at L.

"Ayo, word to my mother dats dat dark blue Lincoln third time riding through here".

L looked at the Lincoln, then looked back at Hav.

"Ayo, who be driving dat joint".

"I don't know"

"Ayo Kaboom, go and grab da chopper from outta Uncle Sam basement and sit dat bitch right here in da bushes".

"Shitd, dat joint is already on da side of da house, I been snatched dat joint up. It's been a little too much traffic around his muthafucka". Hav looked at Kaboom

"Word up"

A smoker walked up to Uncle Sam porch.

"I got 50".

Kaboom walk to the side of the house and waived his hand to the smoker to come over to him.

As soon as Kaboom served the smoker another smoker pulled up in a Buick. Hav hopped in the passenger side of the Buick and served the smoker. When kaboom came back to the porch he looked at L.

"Ayo, it was some hoes in Pete's last night, I saw you getting at that dark skin chick"

L smiled.

"She had a crazy wagon right? Yeah, shorty shit was stupid, but she was playing hardball with a nigga, she wasn't trying to slide with da kid, I was tryna get dat bitch, word up!"

"I saw bro slide off with Shameka ol thick ass".

"Yeah, I peeped his ol sneaky ass"

All three of them started laughing. Hav looked at L.

"Ayo, bro got him a nice laundromat spot up there in the University Plaza".

"A laundry mat spot is a good investment especially if you got it located near a school campus, he gon eat off dat joint".

"Dat's a fact"

Hav looked at L.

"He might not fuck around with da drug game, but da boy is a hustler and know how to get dat paper, word up!"

L looked at Hav.

"Dat's a dangerous nigga I saw da nigga lay on niggaz for months, word up! And his gun game is crazy, he da type of nigga dat you don't wanna war wit because he don't really gotta come out to these streets, he already got a business dats doing good, bro is a problem for real he could just focus on taking ya head off, word up tho!"

After Hav served a couple more smokers, he told L that he need to cop some more work from him. L looked at the time on his phone.

"Aight"

L tossed his car keys to Hav.

"I gotta hurry up and play my numbers pull da whip up to the store".

L started walking to the corner store, and Hav hopped in L's Lexus and pulled it up to the store. After L played his numbers, he hopped in the passenger seat and him and Hav headed to one of his stash houses that he owned in the hood.

When they pulled up to the house, L ran in the house to get the work while Hav waited in the driver seat enjoying the air conditioner. L weighed a half a brick on the triple beam scale, then put it in a big zip lock bag and exited the house.

While locking the house door with his back facing toward the street, L heard gun shots that seemed to be in close range. "Boom Boom Boom Boom", he quickly reached for his 44 bulldog mag that he had on his hip and spun around.

When he was fully turned around, he saw that same dark blue Lincoln MKZ on the driver side of his Lexus with the passenger door window down firing the shots into his Lexus.

Once the dude that was firing the shots into L's car saw L with his gun in his hand, he fired two shots at L. L quickly jumped over the porch banister and started running towards the Lincoln firing shots while the Lincoln was pulling off. "Boom Boom Boom Boom Boom".

The Lincoln quickly sped off. All of L's shots hit the Lincoln, but L couldn't tell if he hit anybody in there. L ran back to his Lexus and saw Hav slumped in the driver seat with three gunshots to the head. Hav was dead right there on the scene.

****

L and Chew didn't know for sure who killed Hav, but deep down inside L felt that those shots that Hav took was meant for him because the shooter targeted L driver side of his Lexus. The first thought about the shooting that came up in L and Chew's minds was that Jac must be striking back.

Word got out that South Buffalo dudes were known for driving that same kind of Lincoln but that wasn't really strong proof that South Buffalo was responsible for the shooting. Truth be told that same kind of Lincoln could be driven by somebody in every hood.

L and Chew needed facts and the only thing they could come up with was that Jack had to go. It was now time to hunt Jac down and kill him. There was no way that Chew and L was gonna let Hav get buried by himself.

L and Chew wasted no time in trying to hunt jack down. Before Chew tied Jack sister up, he was studying all of Jack's whereabouts. L was driving a Dodge Ram pickup truck while Chew was in the passenger seat giving him the directions to all the spots that Jack be at.

After going to a few of the spots that Jack normally be at and seeing no signs of him, L and Chew became frustrated. Both of their blood was boiling, it seemed like Jack got low and went underground.

L looked at Chew.

"Ayo, fuck this cat and mouse game with this old nigga. since he don't wanna come out, we just go knock off his main South Side niggaz and bring him out because nine times outta ten, it was dem niggaz dat knocked off Hav anyway, they da niggaz dat he's feeding so they would be da ones to ride for him".

"I was thinking da same thing too, swing back through dat bar on South Park Street where dem niggaz be at".

"Yeah, let's send Hav some company".

Just like Cold Spring had Petey Pete's lounge to hang out at, it was a lounge just like that in South Buffalo for them dudes to hang out and hustled at. This was a bar that you were guaranteed to bump into a South Buffalo dude. Chew and L already knew most of the main South Buffalo dude's car that they drove. While they drove through the parking lot of the lounge they scanned each car in the parking lot. Chew was the first to notice one of their cars.

"Ok, there goes da kid Ricky's Audi"

Chew pointed to a nice burgundy A8 Audi that was parked

"Yup, dat's his joint"

"Let's hurry up and park dis joint on da side block"

L park the pickup truck on the next street. They both slid on their gloves and put their baseball hats down low and exited the truck. Putting in some work was something that Chew and L did numerous times. They quickly walked over to the parking lot of the lounge squatted down in between a Chevy Tahoe truck right behind the burgundy Audi.

It took Ricky almost 2 hours to come out the lounge. Along with Ricky were two other dudes. One of the dudes was South buffalo main hitter name Kev, who was known for staying gripped up with a gun and putting work in. All three of the dudes were walking through the parking lot laughing and joking around.

When they got close to the Audi, Ricky hit the unlock button on his key and walked toward the driver side door. Chew came charging out from where from he was squatted at. Before Ricky could turn around "BOOM". Chew shot him in the head once

Kev saw Chew run up on Ricky and shoot him in the head he quickly reached for his gun but before he could get his pistol out, L ran up on him from behind and shot him in the chest "BOOM". The impact from L 44 bulldog mag knocked Kev to the ground causing his gun to fall out his hand.

The other dude that was with Ricky and Kev started running and screaming out loud. L started shooting at him while he was running "BOOM, BOOM, BOOM". While L was shooting at that dude, Chew ran up to Kev who was on the ground already looking to be dead. Chew stood over him "BOOM, BOOM". Both shots hit Kev in the head. L and chew walked fast back to the pick-up truck and pulled off smoothly. L looked at Chew.

"Damn, dat nigga got away but I hit him in da leg".

"Dat's even better because now all we gotta do is pull up to da hospital and wait to see if Jac pull up".

L smiled at Chew.

"You right bro".

Right after putting in work at the South Buffalo lounge parking lot L and Chew drove straight to ECMC hospital. They parked across the street where they could have a good view of the emergency exit. Three hours went by without any sign of Jac. They were parked across the street from the E.R entrance and they noticed another South Buffalo dude name Derrick driving his green Grand Jeep Cherokee leaving the hospital. L was the one to spot him out.

"Ayo, is dat da kid derrick's Cherokee?"

"Hell, yeah, follow dat nigga and once he pull up at one of these lights, pull right up on the side of him".

Chew didn't have to tell L twice. As soon as Derrick came out of the parking lot, L was two cars behind him. Derrick approached the red light in the Lane that his driver side was right next to the yellow line that separates the traffic direction. Chew knew L had driving skills and could easily get away from cops in a high-speed chase if one was to happen. Chew leaned up in his seat.

"Fuck dat bro, pull up on da driver side"

When L pulled up on the driver side of Derricks Cherokee Chew quickly rolled his window down. Derrick turned his head to see what was happening, but before he could react "BOOM". The first shot caught him in the face. By time he realized what happened "BOOM". The second shot him right in the head killing him instantly causing his body to jerk which led to his foot coming off the brakes and his Cherokee rolling.

As the Cherokee was rolling "BOOM, BOOM, BOOM" all three shots hit Derrick body. L pushed his foot down on the gas paddle, and they made their getaway.

*** Chapter 5 ***

Hav's killing along with the murders in South Buffalo lounge parking lot, and Derrick's murder all made headlines in Buffalo. People that were in the street game in Buffalo knew that the killings were related.

Once people heard about Hav getting knocked off, they knew some bodies were soon to drop. The Buffalo police turned up the heat and was doing everything they could to get people to talk about those homicides.

They were patrolling Dodge Town regularly and taking people to jail for petty crimes such as loitering, smoking weed, they even arrested people for shooting dice. Chew took Hav's death really hard and he made it his business to hunt Jac down.

There was no sleeping for chew until Jack was dead. Word spread through the streets that it was Derrick that knocked Hav off and come to find out, Jac didn't even order the hit. Derrick took it upon his self to try and kill L once word got out that L had bricks for a good price not really knowing for sure if L had something to do with Jac getting robbed. Derrick knew how dodge town dudes got down and just assumed that it was L and Chew that Robbed Jac. So, to show his loyalty to Jac, Derrick took matters into his own hands. Although Jac didn't order hav's hit, Chew and L still felt that he had to go.

Derrick's funeral was going to be on a Friday. Everybody knew that Jack took care of Derrick so they knew Jac would come to the funeral and show his respect and love to Derrick's family. Ever since the robbery and shootings that's been going on, Jac has been low key and staying off the radar. It was starting to become real frustrating to Chew on hunting Jac down.

For the last few days Chew has been camped outside of the barbershop that Jac was known for getting his haircut at. Today was Thursday and Chew just knew that Jac would be making an appearance to the barbershop. Chew, L and Jay Jay camped outside of the barbershop in a rental car.

This barbershop was not only a popular barber shop in Buffalo, but it was located downtown in a busy area. Usually Chew and L wouldn't do a shooting in this area, but Jac had to go as soon as possible. Jac showed up to the barbershop just like Chew expected.

When Jack entered the barbershop, he had a young dude with him. This was a well-known shop Chew and L knew that Jac wouldn't' be caught sitting in the shop waiting for an open barber chair. They knew that he would have a set appointment so that he could be in and out.

The plan was to have Jay Jay go into the shop like he needed a haircut. Once he saw that all the barber chairs were full, he'll sit down in front like he wanna get a cut in the next available chair, he would then text

L and let L know where Jac and the young dude were sitting. Once L text back that was the code to get up in front like he didn't have time to be waiting for the haircut and walk out of the shop.

The barbershop had cameras and they buzzed people in and out, so as Jay Jay was leaving out, Chew and L would run in there with their masks on and handle their business.

Chew was the first one through the door, he came running in so fast that by time Jac's young boy realized the mask up man with a gun in hand, it was too late. "BOOM, BOOM" the first two shots hit Jac in the body causing his body to jerk but to Chews surprise Jac had on a bulletproof vest and was lucky enough to get a shot off from his gun "BOOM" the bullet just missed Chews face. Jac tried to hop out of the Barber chair "BOOM, BOOM, BOOM". All three shots hit Jac in the face. People was screaming and trying to run out the barbershop, which made it even easier for L to get the young boy that was with Jac. The young boy pulled out his gun and raised it but couldn't get a clear shot off at Chew because all the people in the shop was running towards him.

L came up from behind the young dude "BOOM, BOOM" and hit him in the back of the head. Chew walked over to Jac's body "BOOM, BOOM" and hit Jac twice in the head.

L then stood over the young dude body "BOOM, BOOM". L and Chew ran out the barbershop heading towards the rental car. Jay Jay was already in the driver seat with the car running. Soon as L and Chew hopped in, Jay Jay pulled off.

. . . .

The funny thing about Buffalo dudes is that out in the streets they were quick to fight and kill each other, but in prison they stuck together and held each other down. Before the Feds came and snatched Gator up he was able to put his money up in a safe spot. After blowing trial and receiving 25 to life sentence, Gator had Darlene and Precious open the nail shop, soul food restaurant, and the record store with his money that he had saved up.

Gator had been in Lewisburg Penitentiary in PA for the last 12 years. Lewisburg Penitentiary housed some of the most dangerous dudes in the country. Most inmates that been in Lewisburg for a longtime new Gator and respected him as a real stand-up guy.

Gator had a high-profile case, and in the system, he was considered a real menace to society. The system looked at Gator like he was the kingpin of Buffalo streets. Everybody that knew Gator, knew that he really did have a good percentage of Buffalo on lock, and Gator loved every bit of it, he truly felt that you couldn't mention the city of Buffalo without mentioning his name.

Although Gator was Muslim, he was still considered the big homie of the Buffalo inmates to everybody in Lewisburg. Gator made sure that all the Buffalo dudes that was solid and wasn't no rapist or child molester was alright. If a problem was to occur between the Buffalo dudes and another inmate from a different state or gang, majority of those big homies from that state or gang would talk to Gator first. Other than working on his appeal, Gator was just doing his time and trying his best to keep his hand in on the dope game trade that was going on in Buffalo.

As soon as Gator walked in the yard his little man Curly walked up to him and greeted him. Curly was five years younger than Gator and was also from Buffalo. Curly was serving 20 years for bank robberies. Curly looked at Gator

"What's up?"

Gator gave Curly some daps and a brotherly love hug.

"Cooling, how you?"

"Everything is everything, ya boy got dat paperwork"

"Did you check it out?"

"Yeah, he straight and just like he said, Jerome set him up"

"Gator scanned the yard with his eyes, where he at"?

"He down bottom with da town".

"Aight! Well, I'm gon spin da yard with him and kick it with him. later we gon put together a care package for him".

Chuck was also from Buffalo. Gator knew Chuck since they were teenagers. Back when Gator was home Chuck wasn't too much of a big-time player, he was more of a middleman that ate from setting up drug transactions. Chuck was an alright guy, but even though he was considered alright, and knew Gator since they were teenagers, Gator and all of the other inmates had to make sure that his paperwork was right before they embraced him. Chuck was fresh up on a fifteen-year bid

When Gator and Curly walked up on the Buffalo dudes, Gator embraced everybody with some daps and then him and

Chuck took a walk around the yard. Gator smiled at Chuck.

"Chuck what's up baby?"

"Chuck smiled back at Gator, man, I can't call it"

Gator can tell that Chuck was a little stressed out. "Come on now shake it off baby you here now, so all you can do is just handle dis shit and not let it handle you, feel me?"

"Yeah, I feel you"

"So, Jerome lined you up to dem peoples?"

"Word he was wearing a wire da whole time"

Chuck shook his head.

"And da crazy shit about it is dat it wasn't even my dope, you already know my style. I was just eating off the clip game, he will call me every now and then looking for some weight, I'll find somebody that could hit me for da low, I'll hit him and get me a couple of dollars off it, da whole time he was wearing a wire on me"

Gator shook his head.

"Wow that's nasty work, word up!"

"But da feds already knew that I was just a small fish, so when they knocked me, they tried to get me to flip and work for them".

Gator was paying close attention to Chuck body movements and studying his body language.

"I'm not gon sit up here in front like I'm a gangster because we both know dat's not my style, but at the same time, I'm not a bitch ass nigga or a rat, so I told dem to go fuck themselves and the judge felt some type of way because I didn't cooperate with them and smoke my boots with 15 joints".

"Man, dats just how dis shit go, da system is designed to make real stand up niggaz like us suffer".

"You ain't never lie about dat word up! On real shit tho, other than money and pussy you ain't really missing shit out there, da game is fucked up out there, these young niggaz got da game all fucked"

Gator shook his head.

"I heard! But it can't get no worse than this shit, freedom is everything these crackers got me in here fighting for my life".

"I heard dat you were working on an appeal"

"Yeah, I'm trying to get dat life off my sentence".

"Oh, you heard what happened?"

"What you talking about?"

"Jac just got knocked off".

Gator didn't like Jac one bit, he always felt like Jac was soft and that the money made him, so as far as he was concerned, Jac was better off dead and out of his way. Gator used to hate it when other people would say that Jac had Buffalo on lock. In Gator eyes there was only one King of Buffalo and that King was him.

"Dat's crazy, what da fuck was Jac into out there that caused somebody to knock him off?"

"As far as I know, Jack was always lowkey and under da radar, I don't know too much about dat yet, but later I'm going to call my peoples and find out".

Right after Chuck finished his sentence, a C.O called out, "EARLY GO BACK", over the loudspeaker. Chuck looked at Gator.

"Ayo, I'm about to slide back on da go back".

"I'm gon holla at you later, I'm about to go and get dis money. Oh yeah, I'm gonna have da home team put together a package for you".

"Alright, good looking".

After Chuck left on the early go back, Gator went over to the weight shack where his Muslim brothers were working out at. Gator walked up to Raheem.

"I Salaam alaykum"

"Wa laiqkum Salaa"

Raheem wasn't just Gator Muslim brother, but he was also his right-hand man that he did business with. Raheem was from Newark NJ and was heavy in the dope game, he made millions of dollars off the dope game.

Raheem was originally sentenced to 80 years, but after fighting his appeal, Raheem gave back 50 years. Raheem been in Lewisburg Penitentiary for almost 10 years, prior to him being in Lewisburg, he was in Hazleton Penitentiary for 13 years.

When he got to Lewisburg and met Gator, he took a liking into Gator. Raheem's brother Jahid took over Raheem's business after Raheem caught his fed case. Jahid spent a lot of money for Raheem lawyer to get those 50 years knocked off his sentence.

Once Gator found out about Raheem being a heavyweight in the dope game he sat him down and let him know that he knew some hustlers in Buffalo in the dope game looking for a good connect, and that they'll spend good money with his brother to a point that both of them can make some money off of each transaction .

Raheem was really overprotective about his little brother and didn't really like Jahid dealing with a lot of people. Raheem left Jahid with enough clientele to a point that he didn't need no new clients. At first Raheem didn't want to do that type of business with Gator because he didn't really know much about Gator.

But after Jahid spent all of that money on Raheem lawyer, and the feds did another sweep in Newark, which caused Jahid to lose some good clientele. Raheem did a background check on Gator and other than hearing that Gator was real greasy, everybody said that he was a standup guy that honored the code to the game. Raheem decided to take Gator up on his offer.

Bricks of dope were going for anywhere from seventy to seventy-five thousand dollars in Buffalo. Jahid was letting his bricks go for $60,000 but if you were copping More than 2 bricks, Jahid would let you get it for $55,000. Gator knew some hustlers in Buffalo that would cop some bricks from Jahid for $65,000 which would leave a $10,000 clip for him and Raheem to split.

As time went on those hustlers from Buffalo were copping more and more bricks from Jahid. It got to a point that Jahid didn't have to serve anybody except for the Buffalo dudes. Gator and Raheem we're making at least 20,000 a month. this made their friendship and bond even stronger. As they did their pull-ups on the pull up bar, dips and push-ups they held a conversation.

"I talked to bro today and he told me that ya peoples came and got some more of dem things. So, when you talk to your daughter, she should be pulling you up on your cut. I wanted to tell you when you first came out to da yard, but I saw you spinning da yard with ya Buffalo Comrade.

"Yea, I had to make sure dat paperwork was correct"

"I figured dat"

"Damn, they copped some more?"

"Dats a fact"

"They really out there doing numbers"

"I'm not go even hold you up, I didn't think dat y'all Buffalo cats were really out there getting it like dat because when you mention New York State, people seem to only think about New York City, but now I'm a witness to y'all Buffalo cats getting it in too".

"Ayo, don't let none of dat shit fool you about Up-State New York, my city been active, google da murder rate and you'll see fa ya self how we give it up. Its real cats everywhere, ya feel me".

"I feel you".

"Just like dem young boys from my town say it, money bags with toe tags and body bags"

Raheem laughe out loud.

"Yeah talk dat talk"

"See, you trying to get me started with talking Dat player shit, but I'm not gon give it to you like dat"

Gator laughed out loud, right after Gator finished his sentence, one of their Muslim brothers walked up.

"Ock, you still trying to get on da Jax?"

Raheem looked at Gator.

"You wanna call ya peoples and see if dat landed?"

"I was gon wait til tomorrow, but you know what? I'm a call now!"

"Aight, just let me know when you get off".

"Aight!"

Gator and Precious had a strong father and daughter bond. In Precious eyes, Gator could do no wrong. Gator took good care of Precious and was very protective over her. Precious loved the respect that her father held. Off the strength of her father, people in Buffalo treated her with much respect and she hardly ever had any problems with anybody.

Precious looked up to her father as a true gangster. When she was 13 years old she remembered her father bringing in three garbage bags full of money into the kitchen and told her that if she could count all of the money that was in the garbage bags, he would give her $2,500. By the time she was finished with the first garbage bag she lost count and couldn't keep up. She never seen that much money up close in person.

Gator said something to her that she'll never forget, he looked her straight in the eyes and said always remember this.

"If you could count ya money, then dat means you ain't got enough and if you ever deal with a man, make sure he got a lot of money like your daddy".

Precious wasn't no gold digger, but she wasn't messing with no nigga, she wanted a man like her father that not only was about getting money and taking care of his family but also had morals and principles that he lived by.

Gator was the best man ever in her eyes. When she got older and got a better understanding of her father's lifestyle, she respected him even more when she found out that her father took all that time without snitching. Gator used to tell her that the worst person on earth was a snitch and to never deal with a snitch.

When Gator called Precious on the phone, she picked up on the second ring when she saw them Lewisburg Penitentiary phone numbers.

"Hey dad"

"What's up Princess?"

"At da shop working hard"

"Ain't nothing wrong with dat, get dat money baby! Did you talk to ya mother today?"

"Yeah, she was just up here, she had to go and pick up some more food for the restaurant"

Pick up some more food from the restaurant was their code for picking up Gators cut.

"Ok, so how business been going for y'all?".

"It's been alright, they opened the laundry mat up again".

"I thought da guy was trying to get rid of that laundry mat?"

"He did! He sold it to this guy named Chew"

"Chew? what type of name is dat? It sounds like a guy from da streets!"

"Yeah, he's from da streets, his friend car was shot up on the news the other day but he's alright tho, he kinda remind me of you"

"Remind you of me? They don't make dem like me no more I'm da last of a dying breed, you can't compare none of dem dudes out there to ya daddy".

"Dad, I'm not comparing him to you, he just reminds me of you".

"It sounds like you've been around this Chew cat".

"Well, his laundromat is right next door to my shop, so I do see him whenever I go in there but other than dat, I don't be around him".

"I hope not because if his friend car was getting shot up, then you don't need to be around him, matter of fact what hood is he from?"

"I don't know all of dat that".

"What kind of car does he drive?"

"He drives an Escalade, why?"

"Because I gotta do a background check on this Chew cat. I gotta make sure dat he's not bringing no drama around my baby girl".

"Dad, you don't gotta do all of dat. I told you he's an alright guy, you could even ask mom, she likes him too".

"Hold up! What you mean she like him too?"

Precious laughed out loud.

"Not like dat Dad, you sound like you got a little jealous when I say mommy likes him too, trust me dad, it's not like dat, he's my age".

"Well, I gotta do a background check up on him, and see for myself if he's an alright guy to be around my family".

Precious knew that Gator could be very over-protective, she was now asking herself why did she even mention Chew's name to her father. To keep her father from asking more questions about Chew, she switched subjects.

"Oh, Dad you remember dat guy Jac?

"Yeah, I remember him, why what about him?"

"He was murdered inside of a barbershop".

"I heard! It's not no surprise tho, because when you living dat lifestyle that he was living, those are just some of the consequences, dat's why I tell you to not even waste your time dealing with any of these dudes dat's in those streets, get you one of those guys dat got a good career, trust me, it's not worth dealing with da street dudes, look at me".

Precious understood where her father was coming from, but the truth is that she wanted a guy just like Gator. She needed a gangsta type of guy.

"I gotta go, I will call you back tomorrow"

"Ok Dad, love you"

"Love you more"

*** Chapter 6 ***

After killing Jac and his little man, L and Chew both was prepared for retaliation. The whole Dodge Town was gripped up with guns out on the block every day. It was a lot of gunners from other parts of Cold Spring willing to ride with Dodge Town.

Since Chew and L had killed Jac and four other dudes from South Buffalo, they felt like it wasn't a need to keep going at them when they had already settled the score they were now waiting for South Buffalo or whoever else that wanted to ride for Jac to strike back. It wasn't no secret that Dodge Town dudes were responsible for Jac's and the South Buffalo killings.

Nobody could just prove it. Everybody knew how Dodge Town gave it up with their gun game and after those recently killings, not too many people would want to get involved with some killers that was putting heavy work in like that, they would rather let things cool off and do a sneak attack.

L and Jay Jay was in the living room smoking a blunt and playing NFL Madden on the Xbox when a text from an unfamiliar number came through L's phone. The text message read.

"Melo"

L looked at his phone and said his self "who da fuck is this?" L paused the game and texted back, "who dis?"

"It's Trina, I thought I saw your car on da news shot up a few weeks ago, so I was just checking up on you to see if you were alright".

"Yeah I'm good! Thanks for being concerned, let me find out dat it took for my car to get shot up to hear from you, Smh".

"Melo don't be like dat, you already know my situation, but like I said before, I just wanted to check up on you and see if you're alright. Take care and be safe".

"Well, if you're really concerned, I'm not alright but seeing you will make me feel better".

L really wanted some of Trina since the first time he saw her at the car wash and if L's car getting shot up was a way to get up with her, then he was going to use it because at the end of the day, he knew that his boy Hav was up in heaven looking down on him smiling and laughing saying "fuck it bro use me if you gotta get up with her".

"Lol, you is something else, smh"

While L and Trina was texting each other, it was smokers coming to the house and being served by Jay Jay.

"It's a nice day outside we can go and have some dinner and catch us a nice breeze down at da waterfront, what's up? you down with it?"

"Dat' sounds nice but I'm sorry I can't do dat with you. It was nice talking to you, take care!" Trina sent an emoji smiling face.

As bad as L wanted him some of Trina, he wasn't going to sweat her, she was playing hardball with him and L wasn't with those kind a games, so he didn't even text her back. When L was done texting Trina, he looked over at Jay Jay and saw him counting his bankroll.

"I see dat you been on your grind lately".

"I'm just trying to get my weight up. I've been out here playing around too long".

"It's all here, all you gotta do is discipline yourself and focus up, word up!"

Jay Jay was now copping a brick and busting the whole thing down.

"I'll tell you what, this what I'm going to do for you. The next time you cop a brick from me, I'm gon toss you out one. If you stay focused and bust dat bitch down and grind hard, you'll be copping three of dem thangs at one time. Trust me, dis shit is easy. It's all about how bad you want it".

"If dat's da case, I should be getting dat brick later on because I'm almost done with dis brick, dat I copped from you a couple days ago".

The bricks that Chew hit L with was almost gone. L was now down to only 5 bricks. L made a good profit and fed a lot of people from Dodge Town, and all over Cold Spring, he was now ready to go down South and find him a real plug that can connect him with a real shipment.

There was a knock at the front door. L motioned his head to Jay Jay to get the door. When Jay Jay answered the door, it was Uncle Sam. As soon as Uncle Sam walked in, L looked at him and shook his head.

"Damn, bout time you got here, I called ya old ass about two hours ago telling you to pull up".

"Nigga I was busy handling some business, fuck all dat, now dat I'm here, what could my services provide for you?"

Jay Jay looked at L.

"He always got some slick shit to say".

"I know! He not gon be satisfied until we fuck his old ass up".

"Y'all niggaz ain't gon do shit, bust a move den nigga".

L and Jay Jay both laughed. Uncle Sam was known for talking a lot of shit Unlike, other smoker, Uncle Sam wasn't scared of them, he knew dat they really wouldn't do something to him.

"On some real shit tho, I need you to come down South with me and help me find us a plug".

"Down South? Uncle Sam shook his head, I'm not about to go all da way Down South when we could go right next door and get da same shit for da same price, or if not cheaper".

Jay Jay looked at L with a serious facial expression.

"Fuck is dis nigga talking about next door?"

"Thank you because now his old slick talking ass is losing me".

Uncle Sam shook his head again and sat down on the couch, he then pointed his fingers to the bottle of Hennessy that was on the dining room table and looked at Jay Jay.

"Pour me a shot of that henny while I breakdown this Buffalo culture down to y'all young niggas"

Uncle Sam took a swallow of the Hennessy and lit up a Newport.

"Do yall niggaz know why they call Buffalo, Western New York?"

"Because we're the western part of New York!"

"So dat means we're da closest part of New York to the Midwest. See, back in the days before Buffalo was big on drugs, it was strictly pimping out this muthafucka, we had some of da baddest pimps outta New York State right here in Buffalo, niggaz was out here laying dat pimping down and we was fuckin with dem Detroit and Ohio players heavy, we formed an alliance with dem, We'll go out there, and they would come out here and we all would go to Canada together and put down some serious pimping".

"Yeah, I understand dat but it's a new era".

Uncle Sam shook his head again and looked at his cup. Pour me another shot nephew. Jay Jay looked at Uncle Sam.

"Damn, what you gon do, drink da whole bottle?"

L looked at Jay Jay.

"I know, but fuck it give him the whole bottle".

"Da players might change but da game always will remain da same, just like we had ties with dem back den, y'all could have ties with them now"

"Man, you crazy! I don't know no muthafuckin body out there in Detroit".

"Shitd, I do!"

"Let me find out dat you tryna line me up, fuck I look like going to Detroit tryna to cop a shipment? Dis nigga bugging da fuck out. Dem niggaz a murder us for just a brick".

Jay Jay agreed with L.

"And for a shipment they'll knock yo ass off too".

"Dat's a fact and I'm far from pussy, but I'm not dumb either. I'm not about to play myself like dat".

Uncle Sam looked at L with a serious facial expression.

"Nephew you forgot dat I was getting money out here too? I'm da one dat started dis shit around here, listen man, I'm gon take you to Detroit and introduce you to some real official heavy weight niggaz dat could change ya life".

L did remember back in the days when Uncle Sam had the hood jumping for real, he knew that Uncle Sam had to know some heavyweight players. Although, times have changed, and things were a lot different now, he was willing to chance the Detroit trip with Uncle Sam.

"Give me a day to think about it and I'll let you know something".

Uncle Sam went into his pocket and pulled out $50.

"Well, make sure you think about it, now hit me off with something for this nifty fifty".

After serving Uncle Sam, L grabbed his rental car keys and looked at Jay Jay.

"Come on bro let's hit the block".

****

Chew weed house was a well-known weed spot and mostly everybody knew that it was his house, if anybody wanted to retaliate on Chew for Jac's and those South

Buffalo killings, they will most likely try and retaliate at his weed house.

For the last two weeks since Jack's killing, Chew been at the Weed House waiting for anybody to chance their luck with him. Chew was posted up right across the street from his weed house on Flash porch with his AK47, that held 100 rounds in the clip watching every movement while Snoop was in the Weed House serving customers through the backhall way window. Flash was out and about taking care of the laundry mat and all the other legit business that Chew had.

The van service was now bringing in good money since Chew copped that new charter bus, the vending machine business was still doing good, and the laundry mat picked up real fast. Chew was making good money and having more money than a lot of drug dealers.

While he was posted up with the chopper on flash porch, L pulled up in a rental car with Kaboom and Jay Jay. All three of them were strapped up with guns. L walked up to Flash porch and greeted Chew.

"Respect to da gangster".

"Respect"

Chew gave all of them some daps and a brotherly love hug. Jay Jay went inside the weed house to chill with Snoop. Chew, Kaboom, and L stayed outside posted up and sipped on some Hennessy. After an hour L, Kaboom and Jay Jay left to go back to the block.

Now that Chew was a little tipsy, he was now craving for one of those soul food dinners. It's been weeks since he's been up to the laundry mat. Chew asked Snoop if he wanted a dinner and hopped into his black Cadillac XTS. Ever since the killings Chew put the Cadillac Escalade up and been driving the XTS.

Chew was hoping that the retaliation for Jac and those South Buffalo dudes came so he could put his work in and get back to the trenches doing what he does best. Chew was ready to start a new project and catch him a dope boy. As he drove to the University Plaza with his gun on his lap he was blasting Tory lanes and wrapping the lyrics feeling every word.

"All I'm trying to do is hit a lic and put my dogs on, big time chuck that money up until it's all gone, 20 niggas 100 chains, bitch we all on, we all on, we all on, we all on, we all on, so I'm getting shooters because we all on, I got 40s in the Ruger's when we all on"

When Chew pulled up to the laundry mat other than a Kevin Hart poster in the window for his upcoming comedy show in Niagara Falls everything looked the same. Chew walked into the laundry mat to make sure everything was still running smooth.then he went down to the soul food restaurant to order him and Snoop some fish dinner. When chew walked in the restaurant, Darlene was at the counter smiling.

"Hello there, haven't seen you around"

Chew returned the smile

"I had to catch up on some rest and give my body a break".

"You too young to be talking about giving your body a break".

"I'm a hard-working young man".

Darlene smiled at Chew

"I wish we had more young black men working hard like you, half of these young men out here don't even know what hard work is".

"Yeah, It's a bunch of them lazy ones out here"

To switch up the subject Chew ordered a loganberry and placed his food order, and then sat at one of the tables.

While sitting at the table waiting for his food, Precious walked in and went straight to the table that Chew was sitting at. She stood in front of him with her right hand on her hip.

"Chew, where have you been?"

Darlene was in the kitchen just finishing up Chew and Snoops dinners when Precious walked up to Chews table. When she heard Precious question Chew, Darlene look at Precious like she was lost. Chew looked up at Precious like she was crazy.

"Since when have I started owing you an explanation on my whereabouts?"

"Chew be honest, was it my father dat got you not coming around here?"

Chew was now really lost, he looked at Precious with a serious facial expression.

"Your father? What you talking about?"

"I know that my father could be overprotective, but if he had somebody scare you off from being around here let me know".

That impression that Precious first gave Chew about her thinking that her father was some type of God, and that she thought she could do whatever she wants because of who her father was, now was really coming to light. It seemed like the more he talked to her the more he realized that she was one of those females that used her father's reputation and sexy looks to try and flex her muscles. It was now time to set something straight with Precious.

"Ayo, let's get something straight, don't get me wrong, I know that ya father's a legend out here in these streets and that you think dat he's some type of God or something, but you got me fucked up if you think dat another a nigga dat bleed like me could ever run me off. It's not a nigga breathing that could ever run me away from getting my money. I don't give a fuck about what ya pops did or is doing. Trust me, I'm with all dat type of shit, matter of fact the next time you talk to ya pops, tell him everything dat I said, and if he wanna see what's good with me, tell him to send his best shooters".

Chew then stood up and walked to the counter where Darlene was waiting with his food and pulled out a big knot of money, and told Darlene to keep the change.

"Thank you sweetie, and have a nice day".

"You too".

Chew then walked pass Precious looking her up and down like she must've lost her mind. Usually if anybody said anything about her father, Precious would check them right then and there. She loved her father to death and knew that Gator was a real gangster, but it was something about Chew's serious demeanor that Precious could tell, he wasn't for games. As Chew was walking out the restaurant Precious tried to apologize

"Chew, wait."

Her words fell on deaf ears. Chew ignored her and kept on walking. Once Chew was out of the restaurant Darlene looked at Precious with a confused facial expression.

"What was dat all about?"

"You know how overprotective my father could be, when I was talking to him on the phone, I told him that Chew was the new owner of the laundry mat, he started talking about he gotta do a background check on Chew. So, I thought he had somebody scare Chew off".

Darlene shook her head.

"I don't know what got you thinking that your father is the toughest guy girl everybody is not scared of your father. If you look deep into Chew's eyes, you will see dat he's not one of these push over type of guys and behind his sweetness, it's a dark side to him. Trust me, he's not scared of ya father".

"You right ma, because there's something about his demeanor dat reminds me so much of my father".

"And dats exactly what got you liking dat boy".

Precious looked at her mother like she was crazy.

"Girl, I don't know why you looking at me like that, you think I don't know dat you feeling Chew?

"I'm not feeling Chew"

"You think, I don't see how you look at him? girl don't forget dat I was once your age, you know like I know dat you like you some Chew, you just going all about it da wrong way, you so use to these other thirsty boys always up in ya face trying to talk to you, dat you don't know how to approach a guy that's not thirsty like dem other guys, and dat you really like".

Precious started smiling and laughing.

"It's something about Chew Ma".

"He's a handsome young fella dat seem to have a good business side".

"I know right? And I could tell dat he's also in the streets too".

Little did Precious know, Darlene already knew about Chew and his reputation in the streets, she knew that he was responsible for Jac's murder. Darlene was no stranger to the streets, she was a kingpin's wife. Precious looked at her mother.

"He probably don't even wanna talk to me again"

Precious shook her head

"Baby, when you a bad bitch, you can get anything you want, sometimes you just gotta address the situation like a real bitch. See, when you come across a real man, you can't be pulling them sideways little girl stuff, you gotta come straight real at him, them real brothers like it real and straight up".

*** Chapter 7 ***

The trip to Detroit paid off how Uncle Sam predicted it would. L was shocked to see the love Uncle Sam received in Detroit. A lot of old school players and hustlers were happy to see Uncle Sam. It didn't take long for Uncle Sam to connect the dots and find L a plug.

To L surprise the prices were cheaper than Down South prices. L was back in business with a consistent plug. This was something that he was striving for since he first got into the drug game.

Now that he had a consistent plug, L wanted to start buying more property. It was time to step up his legitimate hustle game. While L was in Detroit plugging, a big federal sweep went down in North Buffalo. The North Side was known for selling dope, they had their few crack dealers, but they were mainly known for pushing that dope. A lot of the Hustlers from over there made millions of dollars from the dope game.

When L came back to Buffalo and went to the house auction, he saw a decent house in North Buffalo that was for sale. Cold Spring compared to North Buffalo was the slums. People would rather live in North Buffalo then live in Cold Spring. At first L was going to rent the North Buffalo house out, but after the big federal sweep and Dodge Town hood being so hot over the killings, L decided to set up shop out the new house in North Buffalo.

This would be his first time setting up shop outside of his hood. North Buffalo was never really a crack hood, so L didn't see it as if he was stepping on other hustlers from that hood toes, and if he was stepping on somebody toes, he didn't really care because he truly felt that if it came down to some gunplay that North Buffalo dudes wouldn't be able to stand a chance with their gunplay. Dudes like Tyeshawn, which L considered soft was North Buffalo main hitter, and he was now caught up in that big federal sweep.

L knew exactly how to get the new house jumping. The first thing he did was move Uncle Sam into the house and let Uncle Sam go to work with turning the house into a smoke house, and a place for hoes to turn their tricks at. Within a short period of time the house was jumping. L let Jay Jay and another little homie from Dodge Town work the house with Uncle Sam.

Ever since Hav was murdered in L's Lexus, L still haven't copped him a new vehicle, he was still switching up rental cars. Today he was in a black SRT Dodge Challenger. When he pulled up to the new spot in North Buffalo and exited the car, L noticed Tyeshawn's 750 beamer slowing up as it got closer to him.

L gripped his gun that was on his hip, once Tyeshawn's car was right in front of him, the passenger window came down. L noticed that it was Trina driving Tyeshawn's beamer. At first L was thinking to himself,

"Damn how da fuck dis nigga out already".

"Melo, what you doing in my neck of da woods?"

L smiled at Trina.

"I'm international baby, I thought you knew"

Trina laughed out loud.

"I hear dat hot shit".

It was another car behind Trina. To avoid backing the traffic up, Trina pulled over. L walked over to where Trina was pulled over at and continue talking to her. Trina looked at L.

"I started to call you da other day"

"Well, what stopped you?"

"I know dat you a playa, I didn't wanna interrupt you and step on the next chicks toes"

"Funny! Real funny, I see you got jokes".

"You know you a playa"

"I don't know what you're talking about, but damn all dat, what's up? You still playing hardball with me or what?"

"You keep acting like you don't already know my situation".

"Just think about it, how real could ya situation be if you talking to me right now? Isn't dis still a penalty on your behalf?"

"Melo, don't go there"

L laughed out loud.

"Now its Melo don't go there"

While L was talking to Trina a smoker walked up to him with some money in her hand.

"I got 25"

L look at the lady.

"Go see dem in da house"

L target his attention back to Trina.

"Well I got things to do, but what you doing later? Around 10?

"I don't have any plans for later or 10:00 o'clock".

"Good, we could finally get up then"

"Is you asking me? or telling me?"

L smiled at Trina.

"Just be ready and call me at 10"

Trina smiled back at L.

"Maybe I will, maybe I won't, I guess we'll find out at ten. right?"

While L was backing up from the Beamer, he looked at Trina and shook his head.

"Yeah, I see dat you play a lot of games."

Trina kept a sexy smile on her face.

"Oh trust me, I'm not into games at all".

"Yeah yeah, I'll see you at ten!"

L then walked into the house. When he got into the house Jay Jay and Phats were on the couch playing the Xbox, while Uncle Sam and the smokers were in the basement getting high. Jay Jay looked at L.

"Respect to the gangster."

"Respect"

L gave Jay Jay and Phats some daps and a brotherly luv hug.

"Uncle Sam got the spot jumping already".

Phats looked at L.

"It's good money over here"

"Dat's what's up".

L sat down in a chair and pulled out a Dutch Master, L started gutting it out so he could roll up his weed. Uncle Sam came upstairs to the living room with $70 in his hand.

"Dis bitch Tammy got a cracker down here with a pocket full of money, da man is open like 7-11, he's stuck and spending everything, hit me nice for dis $70.00 so we could keep this cracker open and spending all his money".

Uncle Sam smiled at L.

"Yeah, I got dis muthafucka jumping like da carter in new jack city. Fuck you talkin bout nigga"

L couldn't do nothing but laugh. One thing about Uncle Sam he knew how to get a spot jumping.

"I'm telling you this now, within 90 days they gon be running up in here trying to shut it down because this spot is about to be on fire, watch what I tell you, this spot right here is about to be the money wave, just fall back and let me handle dis shit! Yall niggaz gon get rich".

"Yeah, I hear you talking, but you gotta show me"

"Nigga cut it out, I been showing you nothing but game since you hopped off da porch. Fuck you talking about I gotta show you? Nigga you know how I do".

Jay Jay put a nice piece together for the $70.00.

"Oh, good looking nephew, I'll be back up in a minute"

∙∙∙

Chew and Snoop was at his main house out in West Seneca counting up the plug money for some weed. While they were in the kitchen at the table counting the money, they held a conversation. Snoop looked at Chew.

"Ayo bro, you never fucked with the crack game?"

"Nah, dat never been my lane"

"Why you never thought about just selling weight?"

"Dat's not my style, other than this weed game, I don't sell no drugs".

"I notice dat! As long as I've known you, I have never saw you sell some work".

"To be honest with you, if pops would have never fucked around with dat shit, not only would my mother still be alive but I wouldn't even be in this game, word up!"

"I heard dat pops was da truth on dat basketball court"

"Man, pops use to bring people out, word up! People from all over use to come and watch pops play his college games. Dat shit use to be packed".

Chew sat back in his chair and took a trip back down memory lane.

"Me and my mother would be right there in the front row behind his team bench watching pops put on a show da crowd use to be going crazy screaming his name out. I think I was his number one fan, I used to love going to pops games and watching him show out, dat shit fucked me up mentally when he fucked up his career and started fucking with dat shit, word up!"

Chew paused for a minute, you could tell that he was a little emotional.

"I knew shit was real when he started selling our shit in the house just to get high. It was times when I went to sleep and woke up to the TV being gone, my video games and everything that had any value to it was gone. shit was crazy and dat's when I first stepped off the porch, at first, I was just robbing niggaz dat was hustling on the corners. I wasn't really hitting dem for big money, it was just short, a few stacks here and there, but after my mother got killed in a car accident, I went crazy out here in these street, and started running up in niggaz spots. I felt like crack destroyed my family and fucked up my father's career, so, anybody dat I didn't fuck with or have love for dat was selling dat shit, I robbed dem. I hated drugs for what it did to my family. I promised myself dat I would never use or sell dat shit".

In a way Snoop understood Chew and felt his pain because crack is what destroyed his family, he never knew his dad, but crack did a number on his mother and had her strung out to a point that she basically abandoned him. If it wasn't a for Chew and the Dodge Town dudes, Snoop would have starved to death as a kid. Chew looked Snoop in the eyes.

"Man, crack destroyed a lot of families, Dat's why I really don't understand why niggaz would even sell dat shit, look at you bro, look what crack did to ya moms, na mean".

"You right!"

"Dat alone should have you not wanting to even think about selling dat shit, word up!"

"It's crazy because I never really looked at it like dat, word up! So, you never felt some type a way about L and niggaz from da block selling dat shit?"

Chew looked at Snoop with a serious face.

"Ya see, in dis game there's no right or wrong, da game is da game. Some niggaz a hustle hard by selling drugs to get what they need and want, some a con to get what they need and want, some niggaz a rob and steal. When you living a life of sin, you can't point your finger at da next man. Every one of those players dat I just mentioned happens to be playing their position in dis game. Actually, I'm wrong just as much as L is wrong. So, therefore it's no finger pointing for us. Understand this, you got drug dealers dat will throw dirt on a stick up kid because a stick up kid don't hustle hard to get what he want and need, he rather Rob a drug dealer, but in reality the drug dealers just as foul as the stick up kid because he'll sell drugs to a Pregnant lady, he'll sell drugs to a smoker dat's tryna sell all of da food stamps dat was really meant to feed da kids and won't have no sympathy. So, why is da stick-up kid wrong for robbing him for money dat he just basically robbed from da kids, feel me? But to make a Long story short, I respect da game itself. I can't judge none of us for playing da position that we're good at playing in dis game. I just know my position and my morals and principles to dis shit".

"Now dat you broke dis shit down to me, I feel just like you bro"

"Remember, dat at da end of da day it's all about one thing and dats dis muthafuckin money. Get dis money! Hustling don't just mean selling drugs, hustling means going hard at what you do to generate money. Learn how to invest your money into legit shit. As time goes on I'll school you to dis shit, you already know dat as long as I'm alive I got you".

"I appreciate it bro, because if it wasn't for you looking out, and holding me down, I don't know where I'd be or what I'd be doing. You basically saved my life, word up!"

Right after Snoop finished his sentence, Flash walked into the house. Chew looked at Flash.

"What's up pops?"

"Another day"

Snoop looked at Flash.

"Pops, what's up?"

"Oh, you da man dat I wanna see. I talked to da dealer, he's supposed to be getting a money green Dodge Charger".

Snoop smiled at Flash

"Oh yeah, I'll fuck with dat!"

"Well, once he get it, we'll stop by and check it out".

"Cool"

Chew went into his bedroom and came back with two guns. He kept one for himself and gave Snoop the other one. Flash took the van key off his key chain and gave it to Chew. Chew reached in his back pocket and pulled out his Cadillac Escalade key and gave it to flash.

"Pops, I'll hit you up when everything is straight".

"Alright, y'all be safe".

"Yup"

Chew grabbed the duffel bag that was full of money and all three of them exited the house. Flash hopped in Chew's Escalade and went his way. Chew hopped in the van, while Snoop hopped in Chew's Cadillac XTS and followed behind Chew.

When Chew parked the van inside the Jamaicans car wash parking lot he hopped out of the van and locked the van up and waited for Snoop to park the XTS. Although Chew have been dealing with these Jamaicans for over a decade, and doing good business with them, he still made sure that whenever he plugged from them that him and snoop was gripped up. After Snoop parked the XTS the both of them walked into the office of the car wash. A Jamaican guy looked at Chew.

"Wha gawn brethren"

Chew reached out his righthand fist to connect with the Jamaican guy fist.

"Respect"

Chew then sat the van key on the top of the office desk.

"Every ting crisp ma-yout?"

"Everything Crisp brethren, da van is parked outside with the money in it".

"Cool! Me say about five o'clock".

"Aight, I'll swing back through at 5"

After giving the Jamaican guy another pound with his fist, Chew and Snoop left the car wash and hopped into the XTS. Since they had a couple a hour to spare before the shipment was ready, Chew dropped Snoop off at the new spot in North Buffalo with Jay Jay while he chilled at the laundry mat.

Chew haven't been to the laundry mat since he had words with Precious, so he felt like it was time to start being back up there making his presence felt.

Chew was standing by the snack vending machine when Precious came walking in the laundry mat. As she started walking up towards Chew he said to himself, "Dis bitch keep coming at me with dat bullshit"

"Chew, can I talk to you for a minute?"

Honestly, Chew didn't want to talk to precious and was about to check her for the last time, but due to da fact that it was some customers in the laundromat, he didn't want to cause a big scene at his place of business. So, to keep things smooth he decided to step outside and hear Precious out.

If she got out of line, he was going to put her right in her place for the final time.

As they walked outside of the laundromat Precious walked in front of Chew so he could get a good view of her nice fat round butt. She knew exactly what she was doing. When they got outside of the laundry mat Precious looked Chew straight in the eyes.

"First and foremost, I wanna apologize to you for coming at you like dat da other day. I didn't mean to offend you. Da truth is dat I like you being around so when I didn't see you around, I thought dat my father was the reason why you weren't around, because of how overprotective my father can be. Trust me I could tell from your demeanor dat you are far from one of those pushover guys and dat you ain't having it".

Precious smiled at Chew, then she stuck her right hand out for a handshake.

"Is my apology accepted?"

Chew smiled back at Precious, he was shocked at how she just came at him. Usually, females had a problem with admitting their wrong. This was actually the first time that Chew saw a female stick out her hand for a handshake. Chew had no choice but to accept her apology. His right hand met her right hand, and they shook hands.

"Ya apology is accepted"

"Good, because I would like to make it up to you".

Chew laughed and smiled at Precious.

"So how you gonna make it up to me?"

Precious smiled back at Chew. T

"Tonight, is da Kevin Hart comedy show and I got 2 tickets, we could go there, catch a good laugh and start all over again on a good note".

"Oh, you saying start over on a good note like you plan on starting something with me!"

"We're business neighbors, so we gotta be on good terms with each other".

Chew wasn't really the out and about type of guy, but since he was looking for a new project, he knew that a lot of hustlers will be at the Kevin Hart Comedy Show, which would be a good place for him to key in on a new lic to hit"

"Dats cool with me, we can do dat and more!"

Precious couldn't help but smile and laugh at Chew's response. Everything went smooth just like her mother told her. All Precious could say to herself was, "Yeah the power of being a bad bitch is something special".

"Well, da show starts at 10:00 o'clock, but I'm trying to get there a little before dat and help my mother out, so how about we meet up around 8:30?"

"I'll meet you here at 8:30"

"Ok, and don't be late!"

"I'm always on time"

Precious smiled at Chew and headed back to her nail shop. Chew was just watching her big ol butt shake every time she took a step. Precious looked back at chew and caught him looking at her butt. She playfully gave him a screw face.

*** Chapter 8 ***

As usual Trina was looking sexy, she had on a white net Gucci wife beater with the Gucci print in black letters and a black sports bra with some skin-tight black jeans with some black pumps on her feet.

L wanted to take Trina down to the Marina part of the waterfront and chill out, but so much money was coming from left to right that he wasn't trying to miss out on a dollar. So instead of taking her down to the Marina, he just let her ride with him around the hood while he hit his weight lics. While they drove around in cold Spring smoking and drinking they were listening to some "Meek Mill".

"Yall niggaz playing games I'm really getting mad money just to

commentate, peep how I operate, I put ya chick up in dis ghost bet

she'll cooperate, I'm really balling tear da mall up in and outta state,

been getting money for a while now, I don't know how to hate"

The both of them was listening to the music feeling nice and tipsy. Now that trina was tipsy, L figured that now was a good time to pick her brain. L turned the music down and smiled at Trina.

"What up sexy?"

With her eyes looking a little glossy and Chinese, Trina smile at L.

"What's up Melo?"

"So, why you been playing hardball with me?"

"Because of my situation!"

"Let's be real. if ya situation was so real, we wouldn't have never talked to each other in the first place".

"Right! And you just said the keyword words".

Trina took a puff from the blunt and passed it to L and took a sip of the henny that was in her little clear plastic cup.

"I know dat you're used to these bitches out here just throwing da ass to you, so when you come across a lady, you expect dat same thing to happen with her, but I'm not dat type of chick".

L was listening to Trina, while saying to himself, "Oh really bitch, you know dat you're just like the rest of these hoes".

"I know dat I might look like these other chicks to you because of how I was looking at you at da car wash, and took ya number that day at Petey Pete's, but it's a reason for that!"

Right when Trina said that it was a reason for that, L lifted up in his seat and smoothly slid his gun over from the side of his arm rest to his lap thinking that what Trina just said sounded more like she was lining him up. Trina wasn't slow at all and picked up on the vibe, and noticed the change in L's body language

"Relax, I don't mean it like dat"

Still on point L look at Trina.

"I'm just tryna figure out, which way you mean it?"

Trina took another sip of henny and took in a deep breath like she was reliving something dat she was holding in, and then she spoke in a serious tone.

"I've been dealing with Tyeshawn for almost 8 years. I'm talking about before da money and everything, back when he was spoiled and into sports and yeah at first I'll admit dat I was in love with dat man, but when he got into da streets and started getting money, he became a totally different person".

L already knew Tyeshawn and just like Trina was saying, Tyeshawn did change. So,

L knew Trina was speaking some truth because when L first met Tyeshawn, he wasn't in the streets, he was more into sports.

"He became abusive and real disrespectful putting his hands on me and fucking my friends behind my back".

From the way Tyeshawn was talking to Trina that day in the car wash, L could tell that he was putting his hand on Trina. So, far her story was adding up, and L was seeing some truth to it.

"My family hated Tyeshawn so bad that they disowned me for dealing with him and once they turned their backs on me, he was all I had! And to be honest with you, I never worked a job because he took care of me, which I should've did because by me not working a job or having my own hustle it had me relying on him. So, whenever he did those foul things to me, he called himself making it up by showering me with gifts, but dat couldn't take away the pain that he was causing me. I found myself in a situation where the choice was either deal with the disrespect and be taken care of finically or leave, and find a way to provide for myself. Now we're talking about the finer things in life, so for a bitch to leave dat and go back to struggling, dat's a hard decision to make, and I'm just being real! But as time went along the pain started taking a toll on me. It got to a point dat it just hurt me to even look at him. It's like you hate a person so bad Dat it disgusts you to even look at them, and you can ask any nigga out here if I ever cheated with them on Tyeshawn. I never talked to another nigga or anything. I was a loyal good bitch to him. I swear you da only nigga dat I ever looked at and took their number".

"So, what makes me so different from the others?"

"To be honest, it was good timing, because like I said before, it got to a point dat it disgusted me to even look at him. So, to avoid myself from looking at something dat disgust me, I looked elsewhere, and it just so happened dat when I did that, I found something that caught my attention. Let me explain something to you. Now, don't get me wrong because you got a lot of bitches out here dat could have a good nigga taking care of them and treating them good but they would still go out there and cheat with da next nigga dat really don't give a fuck about dem, but it's also some real bitches out here dats loyal to their nigga and will stick by his side though thick and thin. Through all da bullshit I stuck by dat man side and never stepped outta our relationship, he took a good bitch for granted and when you take a good bitch for granted and make her open her eyes to da point that she can't even stand looking at you, you make her eyes wander elsewhere,and dat day at da car wash, when I was with him, I was doing everything dat I could to avoid looking at him and then you pulled up looking all good and you caught my attention, but if he wasn't putting me through years of pain no matter how good you looked when you pulled up, my eyes and heart would have been with him, if you noticed dat even when I did get your number, I didn't call you or get up with you because even though me and him wasn't on good terms, I was still with him and wasn't gonna cheat on him".

L dealt with so many females that he just knew all of their game. It wasn't impossible for a female to be able to run game on him at this day and age but if she did run game on him then she had to really be a sharp female.

L listened to Trina and studied her body language. He could see the pain in her eyes and could tell it wasn't game that she was trying to run on him. L understood her situation because most guys that were in the street game getting money did seem to take advantage of a good woman and sometimes a guy could cause so much pain to a good woman that it made her vulnerable to a point that she can get swept up by the next real man that's in her presence and nine times out of ten, when that does happen it's because the pain he caused her to not want to look at him, and her eyes will start to wander catching the attention of the next man.

Although he was now getting a better understanding on why Trina was playing hardball, he still wanted to learn more about her to see if he was reading her correctly. Their conversation was interrupted by his phone going off. When L answered his phone, he paused for a minute and all he said was six words on the phone "Aight I'm about to pull up" and ended the call. L looked at Trina.

"On some real shit tho, I feel you and dat's understandable".

L smiled at Trina and winked his eyes at her, and turned the music back up.

L took a sip of henny from his cup and headed to Ada Street, which is another hood in Cold Spring. While they drove they both vibe to the music that was playing. It's been a long time since Trina felt this good around a man.

When L pulled up on Ada Street, he pulled up to a house that had a bunch of dudes on the porch. L hopped out the rental car and tucked his gun in his waistline, he greeted everybody with some daps. When he got to Mannie they embraced each other with a brotherly luv hug.

They walked away from the crowd talking to each other. Trina kept her eyes on L while He was talking to Mannie. Talking to L about her situation was like a relief to her. The whole time they were driving around, Trina noticed the respect that L received. Almost every street that he rolled down people would wave to him or beep their car horn at him, she could tell that he was a man about his business from the respect that he received.

After talking to Mannie for few minutes, L and Mannie exchanged some money for drugs. L put the money in his back pocket then raised his right arm up with his fist balled up to the rest of the dudes, and hopped back in the rental.

As soon as he got back into the car, L phone rang again, he answered the phone and said those six exact words again. The bright light in the City made the scene look nice as they cruised the streets.

It wasn't hard to tell that the block was hot with cops patrolling because instead of seeing groups of dudes scattered around, dudes were posted up in between houses. While L was coming down the street, Trina turned the music down.

"I gotta use da bathroom".

"Aight, let me make this quick stop".

When L pulled up, Kaboom walked up to the car and gave him a zip lock bag full a money. L put the money in the arm rest compartment. Kaboom looked at L.

"Niggaz almost shot up da wrong car out here thinking dat it was dem South Side niggaz trying to slide through".

"Y'all boys stay on point out here. I'm hitting corners so if boys need me, just hit me up".

"Aight, be easy because it's hot out here"

Before Kaboom could finish his sentence, an unmarked police car pulled up right behind L and flashed his lights to get their attention for holding up traffic. Kaboom looked at the unmarked police car.

"Damn, dats da boys right behind you".

Kaboom then stepped away from L's rental car. When L pulled the car over Trina heart started pounding because she knew that L had drugs and a gun on him.

Once L pulled over, the unmarked police car pulled over right behind him with the lights still flashing. L smoothly slid his gun from off his lap to the side arm rest, and once he saw the police officer step out the unmarked car, he smiled and waited for the police officer to get close to his rental car, then peeled off fast.

A highspeed chase with the cops was a normal thing for L. Everybody on the block just laughed and cheered L on, they knew that this was something that L loved to do. L really had skills behind a steering wheel. As soon as L pulled off, Trina started panicking and screaming.

"Boy, what is you doing? is you crazy? Oh hell no, let me out. Stop this car right now!"

L whipped the corner fast leaving the police officer, but the police officer was right back on his tail. L was driving the rental car like a professional race car driver whipping corners and passing other vehicles without crashing them. Trina was so scared thinking that L was going to crash and kill the both of them. The pee that she was trying her best to hold, came out.

"Oh my God, Melo please stop and pull over".

All along while L was driving, he was smiling and laughing.

"Chill, I got dis, I'm about to lose him right here".

As L was coming down Whoelers Ave, a big Metro bus was turning the corner on to Whoelers Ave leaving a little space between a park Denali truck and the bus. The space was a real tight fit, but L managed to slide right through the tight space just missing the bus and parked Denali by inches.

As the bus kept turning the space got smaller and smaller leaving no space for the unmarked police car to fit. By the time the bus driver realized that there was a highspeed chase going on and stopped the bus, it was too late. L quickly turned down the next street and made his way to the backyard of an abandoned house that was three houses down from one of his houses that he owned. When he turned the car off Trina was still in shock with pee on her black tight jeans.

"You is fuckin crazy!"

L hurried up and grabbed all his drugs, money and gun.

"Come on, hurry up"

While they were walking to L's house, Trina was still complaining trying her best to walk fast in her pumps.

"I don't believe dis shit, I got piss all on my ass and thighs"

L got to the front door and unlocked the door and smiled at Trina, who was clearly mad. L looked at Trina.

"And you still look sexy"

"Something is really wrong with you!"

L just kept laughing

"Nigga, aint shit funny".

Trina opened her Gucci purse to get her phone while L was putting all of his stuff on the dining room glass table

"I'm about to call me a fuckin cab"

L walked up to Trina and grabbed her phone trying his best to keep a straight face and from not laughing.

"Be easy! We're good now just relax and calm down".

Trina put her right hand on her head like she had a headache.

"What da fuck have I gotten myself into, I don't believe dis shit"

L grabbed both of Trina's hands and looked her straight in the eyes.

"Everything gonna be alright".

L then went into his bedroom and grabbed one of his T shirts and gave it to Trina.

"Here, you could take a shower and put this on while your jeans and panties are in the washer. It's a towel and everything in the bathroom, take a nice hot shower and I'll put your jeans and panties in the washing machine, roll us up a blunt and make us something to eat, just relax ya self, aight?"

Trina rolled her eyes at L and snatched the T-Shirt from out of his hands and headed to the bathroom.

L's phone started to ring, once L saw the caller was Kaboom he answered it on speaker phone. Kaboom was laughing out loud.

"Yeah nigga I still got it"

"You a crazy nigga. I'm just making sure you good, you got da block hot, they pissed off and on out here on shit".

"Fuck em, I'm at da main castle. I need for you to swing through".

"Aight, I'm on my way".

Trina was ear hustling and heard everything that L and Kaboom were talking about, she couldn't believe how L was just laughing at what just happened, he was really crazy, and for some strange reason it was a turn on to her.

While Trina took a hot shower, she couldn't help but wonder how this nigga could have her so scared out of her mind, but at the same time turn her on. This was an adrenaline rush that she never felt before. While Trina was taking a shower, L was cooking up a quarter brick. By the time she got out the shower, L was just finishing up and letting the work dry. Even in just a T-

Shirt, Trina still looked sexy. When she came out the bathroom, L smiled at her.

"I don't know what da fuck you smiling for because ain't shit funny".

With her clothes in her hands she looked at L.

"Where your washer at? I'll wash my own clothes, you got a bitch pissing on herself. I feel so disgusting".

"I see dat you still got an attitude, da washer is in da basement".

After placing her clothes in the washer machine, Trina came back up-stairs. L was now cooking up some chopped burgers and fries, and had it smelling good. Trina had to admit that not only was the food smelling good, but L actually knew what he was doing.

L's mother taught him how to cook at a young age. Trina didn't know too many guys that knew how to cook. As she observed the house she noticed that L had a nice clean house with nice furniture and a big flat screen TV.

Although L seemed to be living a crazy lifestyle, Trina could also tell that he had a sweet side to him. While L was cooking, he also was rolling up a blunt. He looked at Trina

"It's some more Henny in dat cabinet"

"I had enough liquor, you make a bitch wanna go cold turkey, no more liquor or weed, you really need to slow your role down in these streets, you already had me in a high-speed chase and shit! I hope dat I don't gotta worry about any of ya groupie bitches popping up over here while I'm here".

L lit the blunt,

"I don't have those type of problems".

L's phone started ringing again. L answered the phone on the loudspeaker

"Yo"

"I'm at the door".

"Alright"

After L ended the phone call, Trina looked at him.

"I know that you not about to have company while I'm in here with just a T-Shirt on?"

"Here you go again, could you just put the chopped burgers on the rolls while I take care of dis business"

Before Trina could respond, L looked at her.

"Thank you"

When L opeedn the door Kaboom was standing there smiling.

"You a funny nigga, word up!"

"Ayo, they lucky dat I had shorty with me, word da mutha, I would've took them all through da hood having them looking like clowns".

"You got dem pissed off. I feel sorry for whoever is driving a black Dodge Challenger around here"

Kaboom laughed out loud.

"You already know, they is on the look-out for dat challenger".

"I already know, but yo, I need you to do me a favor".

"What's dat?"

"I need you to take this quarter thang over to the North Buffalo spot to Jay Jay".

"Aight, shitd since you got da block on fire I might as well bear down over there with them".

"You might as well, it's picking up over there"

After Kaboom left the house, L and Trina finished smoking their blunt and ate the chopped burgers and fries. Then they went to L's bedroom and watched some TV. Once they got into his room Trina looked at L.

"I hope dat you don't think that you is getting some".

"You just consistent with dat little attitude of your's"

While Trina and L laid in the bed watching TV, Trina was laying on her side with her back towards L. L was right behind her. Right when L started kissing on the back of Trina neck she moved.

"Stop it Melo".

L continue to suck on the back of her neck and started rubbing her thighs. Truth be told, L was right on Trina's spot. The sucking on her neck had her in one of those situations where her mind was telling her no, but her body was screaming yes.

L moved his hand in between Trina inner thighs and started playing with her clit, while at the same time sucking on the back of her neck. When Trina felt L finger touch her clit, her body jumped a little and she moved her butt back on L's manhood. With a little moan in her voice Trina called out Melo.

"Ok, I think it's a little too early for this"

L turned Trina around so that they were now facing each other.

"You mean to tell me dat you want me to stop?"

L noticed while he was looking Trina in the eyes and fingering her, her pussy was getting wetter and wetter. Trina was now breathing heavier moving her body in the rotation that L's finger was moving in. L started sucking back on her neck.

"I just".

Trina couldn't even finish her sentence, she put her hand behind L neck and moved his face up to her and they started kissing. Trina was now wetter than Niagara Falls, L stopped fingering and kissing Trina and got himself in between her legs face first. L was sucking on her clit and fingering her at the same time. Trina felt like she was in heaven moaning out Melo

"Oh my God Melo, what is you trying to do to me?"

After Trina came, her legs were shaking. L lifted-up and while smiling at her, he pulled out his manhood and crawled up to Trina face and put his manhood in her mouth. Trina went straight to work on his manhood. She was gagging on it and sucking the life out of him. While she was sucking L off, he was fingering her pussy.

"Yeah dat's right, suck dat dick"

The slurping noise from Trina sucking L off was loud. L almost bust his nut, but he pulled his manhood out Trina mouth and walked over to the dresser to put a condom on.

When he got back to the bed, Trina was on her knees ready for L to blow her back out. L couldn't believe how tight and wet Trina was. When he entered her, it felt like he didn't have a condom on. He took his time trying to get all of it in Trina, she was moaning and talking so loud that the next door neighbor had to hear her. Trina was trying her best to throw her butt back on L's 10 inches.

"Yeah throw dat ass back"

"Get it, make me throw it back"

L started pounding Trina harder, and she was loving every bit of it.

"Dat's right baby, make me take dat dick".

L started smacking Trina ass and pulling her hair. They had sex in every position until they both passed out.

*** Chapter 9 ***

Chew wasn't too much of the flashy type of guy but for occasions like the comedy show, he made sure he put something on that looked real good. It was a must for him to come with his grown man game. Chew had a reputation of being a dangerous stick up kid, so a lot of hustlers that knew him would keep their eyes on him and put other hustlers on to how he got down, but for events like the comedy show when they see him dressed up looking like money with a female on his arm, they would feel more relaxed thinking that he was just on chill mode with his girl .

Events like this comedy show was mainly filled with an older generation. This crowd really didn't know too much about

Chew, which made it even better for Chew to play close attention to the hustlers. It was a good chance that Chew could also bump into some of the South Buffalo dudes, which was also something that he didn't mind doing.

As a matter of fact, he wanted to show his face so they could get the picture that he's not hiding or worried about them. South Buffalo had a real big area with more sections than Cold Spring and Chew didn't really know all of their faces, but either way, he was on point anyway so if anything looked funny to him, he wouldn't hesitate to let his gun go off.

For the most part his whole purpose for going to the comedy show was to find him a new lic to study, so he could rob them. There wasn't going to be a plain robber, when Chew did his robberies, he made sure he robbed them for the real stash. With all the dope that's been getting sold in Buffalo, Chew knew that one of these big dope boys had to have some real paper for him to get.

Other than his gold Cartier glasses, pinky ring and a Breitling watch on, Chew was dressed in Gucci all the way down to his loafers. He looked like money and like a real boss. When Kaboom pulled up to Precious nail shop she had her dark purple Mercedes-Benz GLE class coupe running while she was locking her shop up. Precious was looking sexier than ever, she was killing them in a Prada skin-tight dress, and the pumps that she had on made her walk turn heads. precious had to have on at least $70,000 worth of jewelry on.

Chew gave Kaboom some dabs, and as he was exiting Kaboom car he looked at Kaboom "

Aight bro, I'll hit you up when I get back".

"Aight, have a good time and to stay on point!"

"You already know"

When Chew got out of Kaboom's car, Kaboom rolled his window down, and look at Precious.

"I got your license plate written down, so if my bro don't make it back, you'll be the first one I'm visiting".

Precious smiled at Kaboom.

"If you know him like I know him, then you ain't gotta worry about him not making it back, I'm just hoping that I make it back!"

Kaboom couldn't help but laugh at Precious response. Chew shook his head. Kaboom beeped the car horn and pulled off. As Chew was walking towards the passenger side of Precious Benz, she smiled at him.

"You look handsome"

Chew returned the smile,

"You don't look too bad yourself"

Chew winked his eye at Precious. Once chew opened the passenger door to Precious Benz, he sat his bottle of Hennessy on the armrest and pulled out his gun. When he sat down in the passenger seat, he sat his gun right on his lap. Precious wasn't no stranger at all to guns but the fact that Chew had it out in the open on his lap made her question him.

"Ok, so what's dat for?"

"This here for our protection, a nigga might not only try to rob us, but how sexy you looking, one of these rich niggaz might try to rob me for you. So, my gun gotta hold shit down. I can't let dat happen".

"Ok, I'm starting to see da smooth side to you.

Precious laughed out loud.

"Dat was kinda smooth how you threw in me being sexy, and can't have nobody robbing me from you, but it's good to see dat I must be something you value because the way you be coming off at me had me thinking it's no interest that you find in me"

"Whatever happened to us leaving the past in the past, and starting off with a fresh start?"

"You're getting smoother and smoother by the minute".

As Precious was putting the gear into drive, she looked at Chew.

"I gotta make a quick stop to the ATM machine, and then we can hit the expressway"

Chew took a swig of his henny.

"Don't worry about the ATM I got enough cash on me to hold us down".

"I appreciate it, but I like to have my own".

"I respect dat, but you with me! I got da both of us".

Chew looked at Precious.

"We could just hit da highway now".

This was the demeanor that reminded Precious so much of her father, she seen a lot of her father ways in Chew, and it was turning her on by the second. She loved a man that just knew how to take in charge and be about his business. While they were riding on the Expressway to Niagara Falls, Precious had on one of her favorite Mary J. Blige songs blasting through the speakers and was singing the song word for word.

"Bad boys ain't no good, good boys ain't no fun, Lord knows

that I should run off with the right one, I love my Mr wrong".

The comedy show was jam packed with people from all over. There were people from Buffalo, Niagara Falls, and Rochester. As soon as Chew and Precious walked in the building, the first person Chew saw was his father Flash standing right next to Darlene.

It wasn't too much of a shock to see Flash at an event like this comedy show because Flash usually went to all the older crowd events, but was crossing Chew mind was how close Flash and Darlene seem to be. Chew was now wondering was his father smashing Darlene on the low or was they really just good friends. It was kind a hard to figure out because people from flash generation were a lot different from Chews generation.

People from Chews generation was more known for messing around. Nine times out of ten, if you see a female and male close like how Flash and Darlene seem to be in Chew generation, they were messing around, but the older generation was different. Chew didn't know what the deal was with Darlene and Flash, but he was now going to play close attention to the both of them.

As Chew and Precious were walking together, Flash and Darlene were smiling at them. Darlene gave Chew a hug.

"Look at you Chew, looking all grown and sexy".

Chew had to catch his self from saying something back slick and sexy to Darlene, she was giving Precious a run for her money with the sex appeal. Chew smiled back at Darlene.

"I be trying".

"Ma, dont let him fool you, he be knowing what he doing"

Flash walked up to Chew.

"Hey son, why you didn't let me know dat you were coming here?"

Chew laughed to himself and was saying to himself, "Nigga you full of shit you just shocked that I caught your ass up here around Mrs. Darlene". Chew looked at Precious. "I'm a let Precious tell you why I'm here on such short notice"

Precious playfully rolled her eyes at Chew and then looked back over to flash.

"Because he was too busy playing Mr. Tough guy and being stubborn towards me"

Chew looked at Precious with a smile and a shock facial expression.

"So, basically you not a woman of her word? What happened to us…"

Chew didn't finish his sentence. Darlene smiled at the both of them and shook her head. It was funny seeing somebody other than Gator that could control Precious spoil rotten ways. Precious looked at all three of them.

"If ya'll excuse me, I gotta get a drink, due to me being the driver I couldn't drink and drive, while Chew was just relaxing and sipping on his henny"

Darlene laughed

"Y'all two is something else"

People from left to right were coming up to greet Flash and Darlene. Everybody that came up to Flash, he introduced them to Chew. It was a lot of old school dope boy hustlers there. Chew could tell that it was a lot of money in the building. It was a few up town and downtown dudes that Chew knew from his generation there.

It was mainly packed with a lot of old school players from Flash era though. It was also some South Buffalo older dudes that

Chew didn't really know by their faces, but it wasn't hard for Chew to figure out that they were from South Buffalo. If you paid close attention to the crowd you can tell by the company that a guy kept, where they were from.

Those older dudes from South Buffalo was checking Chew out and he noticed it. Chew could tell that they didn't want any problems with him. Darlene wasn't lost at all, she noticed the look that Chew was giving them South Buffalo dudes and respected how Chew carried himself. Chew was on point and looked as if he didn't have a care in the world, he sipped on a drink and was just cooling out greeting people that he knew.

A lot of people was looking at Precious sexy self and telling other people that was around them that Chew had a bad sexy thang with him. Precious had almost every guy in the building turning their heads when she walked by. The spotlight was on Chew more in a top boss way, rather than a dangerous stick up kid way, and Chew loved every bit of it.

While everybody looked at Chew as if he was on chill mode with Precious, little did they know, he was just playing that role. Chew really was plotting on the dope boys that were in the building. A lot of old school hustlers were coming up to Precious greeting her with a hug which was something that you expected because of who her father was.

Chew would assume that they would show his daughter some love and respect. What Chew found unusual was how after most of those old school hustlers greeted Precious, she would point over to her mother's direction and the hustles would go over to Darlene and not only greet her, and but would also pass her an envelope. Chew could tell that the envelope had money in it. He was now wondering what the envelope was about and if Darlene was also hustling. It was a lot going on and Chew was playing close attention to everything trying his best to put two and two together.

It was this one smooth old school cat probably with one million-dollar worth of jewelry on that stuck out to Chew. When the old school cat came over to greet Precious, Chew payed close attention to him. When the old school cat walked over to Darlene, Chew picked Precious for information about the guy. Chew looked at Precious.

"He look familiar, I think I know him from somewhere"

"Dat's Smooth from Central Park, he knows your father, you might have seen him with your father before"

All Chew really needed was the area of the person to start his homework. Chew picked Precious for information about a few other hustlers without her knowing that he was fishing for information about them.

Kevin Hart came out on stage and did his thing, he had the whole building in tears from laughing. Kevin Hart put on one good show and rocked the whole building. What shocked Chew was how the DJ shouted Darlene out over the mic like she was a celebrity. Come to find out she was well known for putting together events like this. Darlene was really into a lot of things, and Chew was now willing to find out what she was into.

Meaning that Darlene heard a whole lot about Chew in the streets, she played close attention to him. Darlene really was playing close attention to him because Precious was with him, and she didn't want her daughter getting caught up in the middle of Chew's beef.

Honestly, Darlene felt that Chew knew how to handle his self and protect Precious if something was to go down because she could tell that from the people that was in the building that knew Chew had a look of respect on their face when they greeted him. The look was more like the looks that Gator received when he was home and him and

Darlene was out and about at events like this.

Not to mention that Chew had Flash sneak his gun inside the building. Darlene only knew about that because Flash had to have her sneak it in past security for him. Since Darlene was known for throwing these events, security didn't check her.

After the comedy show it was an after party at this lounge on Highland Ave in Niagara Falls, but Precious knew that the after party was going to be full of people from her mother and Flash generation. So, instead of going to the after party Precious wanted to go to the casino in Niagara Falls, but first she had to meet up with Darlene at the after party. Chew wasn't a gambler, he knew that the after party was going to be packed with hustlers. Chew really wanted to go to the after party and put some more of his plot game down.

While Precious and Chew were walking to Precious Benz in the parking lot, Chew kept his finger on the trigger of his gun. Although he was a little tipsy he was still on point. Precious reached in her Louis Vuitton bag for her car keys and handed them to Chew.

"Here Chew, you drive, I've been doing a lil too much drinking to be driving".

Chew wasn't in the mood to be driving, he wanted to play the passenger seat and watch everything, but since Precious was tipsy and he had his gun on him, Chew didn't want to risk the chances of getting pulled over by the cops and getting knocked with his pistol.

"Aight! I'll drive"

Precious gave Chew the directions to the after party. The drive to the after party from the comedy show was less than 10 minutes. When Chew pulled up to the lounge it was packed to the point that it wasn't no parking spaces in the parking lot or in front of the lounge. Chew knew for a fact that it was some dope boys in the after party. Range Rovers to every foreign car imaginable was parked in the parking lot. Precious looked at Chew.

"You could just pull up in front of da lounge, and I'll just have my mother come out'.

Chew wanted to check out the scene in the lounge.

"Naw, we're going to in there, I wanna have a shot and check up on my pops"

"Well, you da shot caller, so I guess we could do that".

Chew shook his head and laughed at Precious. He found a parking space on a side block near the lounge. Chew looked at Precious.

"You know so far you haven't been keeping ya word about us leaving the past in the past, and starting on a fresh new start"

Precious looked at Chew

"Relax, I'm just checking ya temperature"

"See, dat slick mouth of yours is gon get you in trouble"

Precious gave Chew a sexy look.

"And what kind a trouble is dat? you gon spank me or something?"

Chew pointed his finger at Precious.

"Keep it up, as a matter of fact let's go and have some more shots, I think I like it when you're tipsy like this".

"So, you think?"

Chew smiled at Precious.

"Yeah, like I said, I think because so far you just been all talk".

Precious was putting down a mean walk in those pumps that she was wearing, she had Chew's full attention. When they got close to the lounge Chew called Flash on his phone and told him to meet him outside the lounge. Chew needed Flash to sneak his gun in the lounge for him.

When Chew got inside the lounge, he noticed the old school hustler Smooth was at a table near the bar with a table full of bottles and a bunch of ladies around him.

Chew played close attention to Smooth and he could tell that he had a few of his shooters also in the lounge with him. Right next to the table where Smooth was sitting at were, a few dudes were watching him making sure he was good.

Either the liquor was now catching up to Precious or she was really feeling Chew and quickly became insecure when she noticed the females in the lounge checking Chew out. Not only was she playing him close but she let it be known that Chew was with her.

"I'm telling you now Chew, don't get one of these bitches in here fucked up because I see how their looking at you"

Chew decided to hit Precious with one of her own slick comments.

"Relax, they might just be checking your temperature"

"Well, they fucking wit da right one"

Darlene walked up to Precious.

"So, you decided to hang out?"

"No! Me and Chew was just supposed to be having a shot, but he's so busy being entertained by all these thirsty bitches in here, in a minute he's gonna cause for me to check one of them".

Darlene burst out laughing and looked at Chew.

"Oh my God Chew, what you done did to my baby?"

"I haven't done anything, well at least not yet".

This was the first time Darlene seen Precious really into a guy. Precious have dealt with other guys before, but they never had her feeling insecure like how Chew had her. Darlene could tell that Precious was really feeling Chew. Darlene started seeing her plan coming together.

Precious looked at Chew with a playful frown and hit him back with one of his line as she pointed her finger at him.

"See, dat slick mouth of yours is gon get you in some trouble"

Flash and Darlene both laughed. Darlene looked at the both of them.

"Y'all two is something else, but y'all look cute together".

Darlene then looked at Chew.

"Chew, make sure you take care of my baby"

"Don't worry she in good hands".

Chew then smiled at Precious and wrapped his arm around her waist. Precious noticed some females were watching Chew hug her, so she entertained it more by giving into the hug and smiling. Darlene couldn't stop from smiling at Precious and Chew.

"They look so cute together"

Flash looked at them.

"Yeah, they do"

While Chew was talking to Flash, he noticed Darlene slid one of the envelopes to Precious. Right after Precious received the envelope she walked over to Chew.

"Chew come on, I'm ready to hit da casino up".

"Aight"

Chew gave Flash some dabs and Darlene a hug and then him and Precious headed to the casino. It was also a few hustlers from the comedy show at the casino. Since Chew wasn't a gambler, while Precious was gambling, he roamed around the casino drinking and being nosey.

The liquor was like a lucky charm for Precious, she won $5000. After Precious was done gambling, her and Chew sat down at one of the restaurants inside the casino to eat. The food that they ate was like the last straw because once they were done eating, neither one of them wanted to drive back to Buffalo. Chew didn't want to risk the chance of swerving on the expressway and getting pulled over with his gun on him so he decided that getting a hotel room at the casino was their best bet.

Chew got a room with a jacuzzi in it. When they got to the room they both hopped in the jacuzzi, relaxed and conversate. Chew figured that he could get a lot of truth out of Precious while she was still a tipsy. Chew looked at Precious.

"So, I wondered was it me or da liquor your good luck? Because I see dat you were very lucky tonight at dat blackjack table'

Precious looked at Chew.

"It's called skills, no luck at all"

"I could see it now, you go make me work for my credit"

"I like a working man".

Precious then smiled at Chew. Chew wanted to entertain the flirting that Precious was doing, but he really wanted to know more about Precious and her mother. From the looks of things, everything about Darlene was strictly legit. Chew could also tell that Darlene had a side hustle.

"So how long have my pops been knowing your mother"

"If I'm not mistaken since their high school days"

"keep it a buck, are they fucking?"

Precious burst out laughing.

"I don't think so, but they are kinda close to each other, as far as I know your father just be helping my mom's out with those events. I really doubt dat my mother would cheat on my father. I mean, I really wouldn't understand her purpose, don't get me wrong, I know dat she got holes that need to be filled but at her age, I'm sure dat she could go without it especially when you got a husband dat's taking care of you financially from behind bars".

Chew was now thinking that just maybe Darlene was out here in the streets making moves for Gator.

"What you said made sense, but I gotta keep it real with you, a pretty lady like ya mother could easily get her needs filled in, and I understand dat she's up there in age and all but she might be getting tampered with"

They both started laughing

"Word up".

"I' be thinking da same way too, I tell you this tho, if she is creeping on da low, then she is real smooth because I haven't caught her yet, but then again she know dat she would have to hide it from me because I'll tell my dad"

Chew laughed out loud.

"Oh, so you a snitch?"

"One thing my father taught me at an early age is to never snitch, dat's not in my DNA.

My father would dis-own me if I was to ever snitch on somebody, we take dat snitching shit real personal"

"So, what would you call it when you tell on your mother to your father?"

"Dat's not snitching, it's me being my father's ears and eyes out here while he's in there"

Precious crossed her fingers then she used them as a symbol, me and my father is like this".

Chew was now seeing that Precious was really daddy's little girl.

"I gotta keep him informed with what's going on in our family".

"Oh, I see your daddy's lil baby"

"If dat's what you wanna call it, then I guess you can call it dat, I'm my father ride til die baby".

"I respect dat because if I had a daughter, I would want her to love me as much as you love ya pops"

Precious looked at Chew with a serious facial expression.

"Chew it's something about you that reminds me so much of my father, I don't know what it is, you got a lot of my father ways in you and It really got me attracted to you".

Chew respected the respect that Precious held for her father, but now was the time to set her straight about real niggaz.

"Ayo, I respect how you look up to ya father, and from the things that I've heard about your pops, he seems authentic. When he was out here in the streets, he was handling his business and when he got caught up, he held his head high and didn't fold, much respect to him for dat but at da same time, it's also other authentic niggaz out here dat get it in just like how ya pops get it in, he's not the only authentic nigga dat you will come across me personally, I know dat its niggaz just like me out here in da streets. I don't sleep on no niggaz and I also don't look up to niggaz like there some type a God or something. I say all dat to say this, it's good to have dat respect for ya pops an all, but they didn't stop making official niggaz when they made him, he's in a class of his own and I'm in a class of my own".

"Chew I know dat you might get da impression dat ,I think I'm all dis and dat because of my pops and dat I think he's some type a God or something but it's not like dat, trust me, I could tell dat you're a man about his business and I don't wanna make it seem as if I'm comparing you to my father because dat's not da case. I just always respected my father because beside him doing what he was doing in the streets he was a family oriented guy, he took care of home and made sure me and my mother was always straight, Although my father used to always tell me dat I shouldn't deal with the street guys dat's like him, a guy like him is all dat I ever wanted, when I see you, I see my father ways in you, dat's what I mean when I say dat you remind me of my father".

"Baby you ain't gotta beat around the bush, just say Chew, I'm feeling you"

Chew said smiling at Precious. So far one thing Chew knew about Precious was that not only did she have her own money, but she came from a family with long money. Which is a good thing because at least he didn't have to worry about her always being in his pockets. Truth be told, Chew wasn't really looking for a relationship. In his line of work, he felt that he couldn't trust females and he damn sure didn't want no female knowing too much of his business.

But as he thought about the situation with him and Precious dealing with Precious could open the door up for him to get around more dope boys, he didn't know what Darlene was into on the illegal side but he knew that she was into some illegal things that just might help him get rich.

Chew needed to find out more about Darlene and if playing Precious close is what it took to find out then he was now willing to play her close. He still felt like he couldn't give into Precious so easy and jump into a relationship with her. Chew was willing to make it seem like he just wanted to take it slow with her but at the same time have her opened off his sex game. Chew looked Precious straight in her eyes.

"I can't lie, I'm feeling you too but on a serious note, I don't want us to move too fast and jump into a relationship, I think we should take our time at really getting to know one another, you know first build a friendship and see where things take us from there, me personally, I feel dat majority of relationships fall apart because they skip the fundamentals of building da relationship. Now and days people are getting into relationships without even establishing a friendship bond, when you're in a relationship you should feel comfortable with talking to your girl or man about any and everything, so if you want to put our past in da past and start off to a fresh new start like you say, then maybe we could work on building a friendship by and getting to really know each other to a point that we will be able to see if a relationship would really work".

The liquor had Chew in a zone talking to Precious hoping that she could understand his story. Precious smiled at Chew. Everything that he just said was understandable and made sense.

"I'm cool with dat, I don't see nothing wrong with taking time out to get to know one another like you said"

From the looks in her eyes Chew could tell that he had Precious right where he wanted her. Chew stood up in the jacuzzi reached his hand out for Precious hand.

"Come on baby, let's take this over to the bed"

Precious couldn't help but notice is manhood arise. Precious thick body was looking sexy in the bra and panties set that she had on in the jacuzzi and from the last look in Chews eyes, when she stood up in da jacuzzi and reached her hand out to grab

Chews, Precious knew that she had Chews full attention, she stood up with the help from Chew and turned around so Chew could get a good view of her butt and she raised her left leg up in a sexy pose to not only get out the jacuzzi but to also keep Chew full attention.

Once they stepped out of the jacuzzi, Chew grabbed a towel and turned Precious around to face him.

"Here, let me dry you off"

Precious gave Chew a sexy smile.

"Dat's so nice of you"

As Chew was drying Precious off, he couldn't help but to admire her soft sexy body. All Chew was saying in his head as he was drying Precious off was "I'm gon murder dis pussy". When Chew was done with drying her off, Precious reached for a different towel and looked at Chew.

"Here, let me return da favor and dry you off"

Precious took her time and dried Chew off. It seemed like every second that went by, Chew was getting turned on more and more. While they walked over to the bed, Precious walked in front of him letting him get a nice view of her butt as it bounced with every step she took.

When they got to the bed Chew was ready to put his pipe game down but to his surprise when he got up on Precious, she looked him straight in the eyes.

"I don't think dat this is a good idea because sex could bring out some feelings, as bad as I would like to, I think it's best for us to just take our time and build a friendship first, like you were just saying"

Little did Chew know Precious was schooled by a veteran. Although Precious was a daddy's little girl that was closer to her father, Darlene still schooled her on being a bad bitch. Precious now had Chew right where she wanted him, she was dying laughing on the inside and saying to herself "Yes, since you wanna talk all dis take it slow shit, we gon take it slow with da sex too". As bad as she wanted to feel Chew inside her, she couldn't give in. Precious then gave Chew a kiss on the lips

"Goodnight Chew"

Precious turned her back towards Chew and pushed her butt up against his manhood. While she laid there with her eyes close, she was smiling.

Chew couldn't believe what Precious just said to him. She just flipped it back on him with the let's take it slow line, he wasn't going to give up that easy. Chew started rubbing on Precious thighs.

"Damn baby your body feels so nice and soft, I just wanna taste it, let me put my face in dat pussy and eat it real good for you".

Precious almost burst out laughing, she was feeling every minute of Chew lusting for her.

"I thought we was gon take our time?"

"Relax, everything gon be alright, we just going to go with da flow"

Precious moved her butt more on Chews manhood.

"Good night Chew".

At that moment Chew knew that Precious was playing games and he wasn't feeling it, but he kept his cool.

"Chew, I really like you and I'm not looking to just be one of those chicks dat you just be fucking from time to time"

Chew was mad, he didn't even respond back to Precious, she got him real good. Although Chew was mad, he still respected her for how she disciplined herself, and didn't give up the ass like most chicks did.

*** Chapter 10 ***

The conversation that Gator had with Chuck yesterday in the yard about Chew stuck in Gators head. When Gator left the streets, Chew wasn't even off the porch yet. Yesterday while Gator and Chuck was walking the yard, Chuck put Gator on to everything that was happening in the streets of Buffalo. Gator already had a street source that kept him up to date with the streets, but whenever he talked to that source over the phone he talked in codes and couldn't really get all the information because his calls were being monitored. Now that Chuck was fresh from the streets Gator was now able to get all of the details about the streets.

What shocked Gator the most was how Chuck said between them two, the streets is saying that Chew was responsible for Jac's murder. Chuck told Gator that Chew was now one of the most feared men in Buffalo, and that he kind a reminded him of Gator. This was Gator's third time hearing that Chew reminded someone of him.

The first time was when Precious mentioned Chew to Gator which made Gator reach out to his street source to do a background check on Chew. The second time was from his Street source, and now the third time was from Chuck. The way that everybody was talking about Chew was like he's out there in the streets laying his gun game down serious. Although changes come along with time, Gator still feel like he was the King of Buffalo, he just couldn't see another person having that throne.

When he found out that Chew was Flash's son, he shook his head and said to himself, "funny how in life the table turns". Gator knew flash real good. Now that Chew was in the streets making a name for himself and was close to Precious, just maybe Gator could get a chance to meet Chew and work something out where one hand can wash the other and together they can wash the face.

The dope game in Buffalo was now really doing good numbers. Gator and Raheem went from making $20,000 a month to around 50 to $60,000 a month. Although, that was just kibbles and bits to the ones that was really moving the dope, it was still a great profit to somebody that's in prison. Gator could easily calculate the profits that the dudes from Buffalo was making from the transactions that they were making from Jahid.

They had to be sitting on a couple Million of dollar. Gator just knew that if he was home that he would be two times over them. There was no way that Gator would've let them dudes be over him in money. Right now, was considered a perfect time to be out there in those Buffalo streets. Raheem was soon to be released and if Gator appeal was to go through with getting the life off his sentence, he would also be released and have the right plug by his side to really take the streets over and be the King of Buffalo for real

Instead of going to the first run to the yard, Gator decided to go to the law library and see if he could find some good cases that other inmates won their appeal on like his case. Gator now had a new lawyer that was better than the last lawyer. This lawyer was coming up to Lewisburg Penitentiary visiting him and to go over for his appeal.

The main rats that snitched on Gator were now dead, which could be a good part on Gators behalf. The one thing that could really hurt Gators chances of winning his appeal is the fact that he had a high-profile case. Even the mayor of Buffalo wanted Gator off the streets.

While Gator was at the law library, Raheem was in the yard doing his work out on a pull up and dip bar. While Raheem was working out, he noticed Chuck was struggling on the pull up bar. Raheem wasn't the type of guy to just open a conversation with people that he didn't know but since Chuck was from Buffalo and knew Gator, Raheem figure that he'll motivate Chuck on the pull up bar. While Chuck was struggling, Raheem walked over and helped Chuck by putting his hand on his back helping Chuck to pull his body up on the pull up bar

"Dat's right, pull".

After getting in a few more pull-ups with the help from Raheem, Chuck hopped down from the bar out of breath

"Good looking! I'm a little rusty, it's been over a decade since I've worked out".

"Don't worry, as long as you stick to it, it'll come back together and get easy for you".

"I see you and my boy Gator be out here going in on the workout"

"Just trying to keep Dat youth in us, na mean?"

"I can dig it".

Chuck reached out his right fist to Raheem for a pound and said his name.

"Chuck".

Raheem right fist met with Chuck fist for a pound.

"Raheem or you can call me Ock, so you one of those Buffalo players".

"Yeah, I'm from da low"

"I haven't met a brother yet from Buffalo dat didnt swear he was a player"

Raheem laughed out loud.

"Awe man, tell me about it. I already know dat Gator put you on to us players. I'm sure dat he got plenty of player stories to tell"

"Every now and then I get it outta him and be having him talk dat talk, he keep trying to me him how nice he was on dat basketball court back in da days"

"He did his lil one and two thing, but it was my man Flash dat was really da truth, Gator was more of a gangster than anything".

"They do talk about how he was laying his gangsta down out there in Buffalo, he was really a problem out there?"

Chuck looked at Raheem.

"A problem? Man, they had to get dat man off da streets. I'm a tell you like I was telling him yesterday when me and him was spinning da yard, if he would have just stuck to getting money, he would a had one helluva run out there in them streets. Gator let his ego get in the way of his grind, once he started putting his pressure game down, those body started dropping, they had to come and get him off those streets. Gator my man, we go back to junior high school, as long as I've known him, he always been controlling and the static type, he couldn't see nobody else eating good without him, either you getting it with him or you ain't getting no money at all. Now I see dat he's Muslim and getting himself together, which is a good thing because he can't be how he used to be out there in them streets, ya feel me?"

"Yeah I feel you on dat"

Raheem heard a few things about Gator, but nobody really broke it down to him like how Chuck just did it. The way that Chuck just broke it down to him kind a made it seem like Gator was a jealous type of guy with an ego, which is something that wasn't not good for business at all.

Raheem did hear that Gator was a little aggressive and could get a little crazy at times, he was now just hoping that this time that he was doing, have really changed him because as long as Gator kept it strictly good business, him and Raheem could get rich if he's released. It was no room for the jealousy and greasiness. Raheem needed for Gator and him to be on the same page. No side deals without each other knowing, no hidden agenda, nothing except for honesty and good business. This time was a wake-up call for Raheem.

Chuck looked at Raheem.

"Gator is a good dude tho, he just got a big ego, but from me seeing him in here, I could say dat he's somewhat a change man".

After Chuck finished his sentence the C.O announce early go back over the loudspeaker. Chuck looked at Raheem.

"Well, dat's my call, I'll see you around"

"No doubt! You be easy".

"Yeah, and you too".

After Chuck left on the early go back, Gator came to the yard from the library and walked up to Raheem.

"I Salaam alaykum"

"Wa-laiqkum-Salaam, so how did it go at the library?"

"I was fishing, I couldn't really find a case tho, hopefully this lawyer could find some good cases like mine".

"Dat's what they get da big bucks for"

"Dat's a fact".

Gator noticed the sweat on Raheem and seen his chest and arms had a pump.

"Let me find out you started without".

"Yeah, I was out here getting it in with ya Buffalo comrade dat just pulled up, Chuck"

Gator laughed out loud.

"Chuck was out here trying to get it in?"

"Yeah, he was struggling, you know how it be on a startup, but he was getting it in tho"

"Dat's up! Well, let me get mines in then"

Gator hopped up on the bar and did 15 pull-ups and went to the dip bar to do 15 dips. While he working out, Raheem stood by his side and they conversated.

Ever since Trina was in that highspeed chase with L the other night, she been wide open and hooked on to L. Trina was used to being the main girl in all of her relationships, she was never the type to play da side chick. One thing about Trina, she was a ride to die chick. If she was with you, then she was with you and you didn't have to worry about her creeping off with the next man.

Tyeshawn put Trina through so much pain for the last couple of years that when he got caught up in that North Buffalo Federal sweep, it was like a big relief to her. Trina was now finding happiness again and talking to L made her feel better. Trina now had the strength to leave Tyeshawn, and the last thing she wanted was for Tyeswhan to find out about her dealing with L from somebody else, so she decided to go and visit him and tell him everything herself.

When she got to the County Jail, Rina was in for a surprise that she didn't expect. Tyehawn was already in the middle of a visit with one of Trina old friends name Tasha. Trina didn't flip out. Although it hurt her to not flip out, she handled it like a real boss lady and not only did she tell Tyeshawn that he could keep Tasha, but she also told him about her and L.

If Tyeshawn could have reached over and strangle her to death he would've. After causing Tyeshawn blood to boil, Trina got up and left the visiting room.

Tyeshawn was really going through it. He started telling everybody that Trina was a foul bitch and was fucking L all along behind his back, and was really trying to make Trina look bad. Almost everybody that he told this to in return told him, that L had set up shop in his neck of the woods. Before you knew it, word on the streets was that not only did L take Trina from Tyeshawn, but he also set up shop in his hood. This was now making Tyeshawn look bad, and L look more of a gangster.

As L was getting to know Trina more and more he started noticing the ride to die side in her, and started really taking a liking to her. Not to mention that Trina sex game was off the hook.

When Trina came to L crying about the visit she had with Tyeshawn, L told her not sweat the situation, he came up with a plan to see how much she was really feeling him and how much of a real ride to die chick she was.

When the Feds snatched Tyeshawn, he had $100,000 in his presence. Tyeshawn had a good run in the dope game, so L knew that the $100,000 that they caught him with wasn't all his money. Trina was his wifey and ride to die chick, he might've had not let her know where all of his money was stashed at, but he had to let her know where some of it was at.

Trina once told L that she never worked a job in her life and since Tyeshawn had been locked up, she had been doing well for a person without a job and a steady income, so L told Trina to take all of Tyeshawn money that she knew about. L was going to find her a dope connect and she could get up with those dope fiend lic's that Tyeshawn had, and build her own empire.

L already knew that Trina was used to the finer things in life because she told him before that Tyeshawn used to shower her with gifts whenever he did something foul to her, so Trina would expect L to treat her good on the financial side like how Tyeshawn did, but L wasn't getting that dope money like how Tyeshawn was getting it. L was getting crack money, which was still good money and all, but it was nowhere near dope money.

It made no sense to get into a relationship with Trina if it was going to cost L, so L came at Trina like, not only how Tyeshawn should've came at her, but he came at her like how a nigga come at a real ride to die chick.

L told Trina instead of me just taking care of you, and you always just sitting back depending on me, I'm going to teach you something so if anything was to ever happened to me, you could still be straight on the financial side and never have to depend on somebody else to come through for you. Since I'm a boss, then it's only right that I teach you how to be a self-made boss bitch.

Understand that most niggaz is not gonna give it to you like how I'm about to give it to you. I'm going to let you see for yourself the difference between a real nigga and these niggas that claim to be a real nigga.

L never dealt with the dope game, the crack game was all that L knew, and to be honest, he wasn't with trying to get into the dope game. L did realize how rich a lot of dudes got in a short period of time by dealing with the dope game, so instead of him dealing with that game, he was now ready to school Trina on how to hustle in that game.

In L's eyes two hustlers was always better than one hustler. As long as he kept his pipe game down on Trina and constantly showed her that he was a man about his business, it will make it better for him to have her mentally.

L was in his living room at one of his houses around his way when Trina pulled up with two big duffel bags. When Trina pulled up she called L phone.

"What's up?"

"I'm right outside and need help with both of these bags".

"Aight, here I come".

While L was walking out of the house to help Trina with the two bags, he was saying him-self "let me find out this nigga left the mother load with her". When L got to the Beamer, Trina opened the trunk. L looked at both duffel bags

"I'll grab them both, just grab the door for me"

"Ok"

Once L got into the living room, he sat both duffel bags on the floor. While he was carrying the duffel bags, he noticed that one of them was lighter than the other. Trina unzipped both of the bags, and then examine them.

"Here Bae, this one for you".

When L looked in the bag, Trina looked at him.

"Dat's $300,000".

Trina sat down on the couch and started going through the other duffel bag

"And this $350,000 is for me".

L was saying to himself that Tyeshawn had a lot more money than this $650,000, but he figured that Tyeshawn wouldn't let Trina know where all of it was stashed at. L was still happy with the 300,000 that Trina gave him. L looked at Trina.

"This for me baby?"

"Yup, all for you". Trina looked around the living room then back at L.

"So now what?"

L sat down on the couch with Trina.

"Ok, this da plan, put $250,000 of that money up, I'm gon show you a good stash spot for dat, I'm gon have my boy get in contact with his dope connect so you can cop a brick of dat thang off him, and you going to work from there and get this muthafuckin money".

L winked his eye at Trina, and she smiled back at him.

"You sure dat you remember how to step on it and put it together?"

"Trust me I did this over a thousand times with Tyeshawn, I know how to turn a 1 into 2 and if it's fire I could throw a 3 on it and just turn that one brick into 3 bricks.

L looked at her

"Damn those numbers sound good, ok dat's perfect"

"Now you know dat Tyeshawn is about to be having his peoples trying to track me down"

"Don't worry about dat nigga, you with me now! And dis what else I want you to do. Everything except his money, I want you to give everything else to somebody dat he trusts"

Trina looked at L like he was crazy.

"Da 750 is in my name and I'm not giving it up, he could have everything else but I'm keeping da whip"

"Naw, fuck dat! Give dat nigga his whip back because I don't want you running around with me in da next nigga shit anyway, don't worry, we gon get us some v's real soon, but for now tho, we gon play this rental car game, you can't be too flashy when you moving work through these streets, gotta stay low and off da radar".

L reached over for Trina hand, and pulled her closer to him and gave her a real passionate kiss, then L looked Trina straight in the eyes.

"I'm going to put you on to game and make you a boss bitch for real, you just gotta listen to daddy and can't second guess what I tell you".

"I think, I'm showing you dat I'm really feeling you, all I ask from you Melo is to please not make me regret this".

L kissed Trina again.

"Relax baby, you fucking with a real nigga now, you see dat nigga may have treated you good and all, but he ain't put you on to dis game and school you on how to get money without him, always remember this, what one half is worth, da other half should be worth the same amount, if you gon be my other half, then I want you to have just as much as I got, it's a secret to society and from you all I ask for is trust, no G-Money shit, and we go do us"

"Boy you going to make me marry you"

Buffalo and Rochester dudes were just like brothers. When Kaboom did a state bid he was with a lot of Rochester dudes and became real cool with this one get money dude from Rochester name Littles. After completing their bids, Kaboom and Littles stayed in contact with each other and whenever Littles ran out of work, he would come up to Buffalo and cop some from L and vice versa. If Nobody in Cold Spring didn't have no work, L would go to Rochester and see Littles.

Little's older brother was into the dope game. Since L didn't really deal with dudes outta Cold Spring in Buffalo, he contacted little's brother in Rochester to connect him with a brick of dope for Trina.

After Trina got the brick of dope, she listened to L and went straight to work.

*** Chapter 11 ***

Now that Chew had a few dope boys on his radar, it was now time for him to study them. This was the part of the game where Chew had to be patient and very observant. Sometimes it could take months for Chew to narrow down a stash spot. This was a part that a lot of people didn't have the patience to do and separated Chew from them, because it took a lot of time. Chew was schooling Snoop to the robbery game.

Tonight, he had Snoop with him schooling him through the process step by step.

It was 11:00 o'clock at night, Chew and snoop was in a rental car riding around checking out the dope boys hang out spots, cars, and the people they be around. As they were driving around Chew had a Jamaican do rag with the fake dreads attached to it on his head with some sunglasses on. Snoop hair was unbraided with a baseball cap on his head with some sunglasses on. Every now and then Chew would throw a question out there for Snoop to answer to see if he was on point and paying attention.

"So, why do I got this do rag and sunglasses on?"

"To disguise your face, so while we're riding around, they don't know dat it's us in this car".

"Why is it better for us to do our homework at night?"

"Because there's less traffic and easier for us to blend in".

"What if it starts taking longer for us to narrow in on our project?"

"We gotta get deeper and start doing some of the Fed tactics, spending more time following him around and studying them".

"What do you mean when you say da Fed tactics?"

"Bring out the binoculars, start going on their Facebook pages to see where they at, and da chicks they fuck with, snatch up somebody their close to and make them pay that ransom".

"What about our car?"

"It's a must that we switch up rentals every other day".

Chew then smile at Snoop.

"Ok, I see dat you're on top of your shit, when it's time to pull it off, I wanna see how you get busy, understand dat walking a nigga inside of his building is way different from just pulling out and robbing him on the spot, you gotta know how to ease up on him and keep him calm and have him scared at da same time, and not let him panic and blow up da spot, Because if you clap him, the neighbors going to hear those shots, and then contact da police, now da spot is hot and the lic is all fucked up, for da most part, all I could really do is show you da ropes, a lot of this shit ya gon learn from experience of doing it yourself, at least seven outta ten lic's dat you hit is not going to go as you planned it, dat's da lesson you learn for ya next one tho".

Chew pulled up to the back of this bowling alley parking lot where Smooth supposedly get a lot of dope money at. Chew parked far back in the parking lot in between two cars where him and Snoop couldn't be seen but where they could also see every movement in the parking lot.

The two of them stayed parked in a parking lot for almost 3 hours. There was no sign of Smooth hanging out at this bowling alley. Every now and then Chew noticed this one guy kept coming out of the emergency fire exit door going to a new Buick town car that was parked right next to the fire exit. The guy would come out the fire exit door, go to the Buick and then go back through the same doors.

As Chew was paying attention to that guy, he realized that the guy was one of the same guys that was sitting at the table next to Smooth at the after party. From there, Chew knew what was going on. Chew wanted to see if Snoop could put the pieces of the puzzle together. Chew looked at Snoop.

"Ayo, you notice da one cat dat keep coming out the fire exit door?"

"Yeah, I noticed dat he came in and out the door a few times"

"Ok, why do you think he coming in and outta dat door?"

"I can't call it"

"He cool with the owner of this bowling alley, every time a lic come to him instead of coming out the front door to walk to his car where he got the dope stashed at and letting people see him running back and forth to a stash , he playing it off nice and smooth sliding out the fire exit door to go to his whip and then return back to his lic having his lic thinking dat da dope is already in the bowling alley".

"Ok, I see what you're saying. It makes sense, his lic don't know dat da dope is stashed in his car".

"Right! But now do you know why he got his car parked in dat parking spot?"

"Because it's right next to da fire exit door?"

"And because da cameras from the bowling alley building can cover dat side of the parking lot".

"Ok copy"

"Now peep game, if you noticed dat ever since we've been sitting here watching this spot, not one dope fiend came through, da only people that we've been seeing is bitches and niggaz"

"Right"

"So dat means dat these dope boys up here not pitching to da fiends. they only selling weight to other dope boys. So, basically this is a weight spot".

"You right!"

"I'm also sure dat it was some other transactions going on in this parking lot with some other hustlers dat we probably missed".

Snoop looked at Chew.

"So, if dude stash is in his car, then dat's even easier for us because we could just catch him when he come back out dat fire exit door?"

"Of course, we could do it like dat, but dat's only going to be a small percentage of what he really got, always remember dis, fuck da crumbs. it makes no sense in robbing a get money nigga for pennies, we want da real stash, and the stash that's in his whip isn't the real stash. If we were to book him right now, it would only alert the other hustlers and it will start a war for just little pennies, but if we catch him for the real stash and knock him off, its gon take a while for his peoples to put da puzzle together on who did it. See, it all boils down to this, Buffalo is but so big, so it's not really hard to find out things, it's like playing Russian Roulette with your own self when you rob niggaz for their pockets and little stash because it's not worth killing dat person over dat short change, all he gon do is pass it over to you, study ya body and do his homework on who you is and now you sitting back not knowing dat he's really coming for you skip all of dat bullshit and just do ya homework correctly and catch him at his house and get everything, once you got him for a nice amount and realize that he's playing with real money, knock him off right there, so he can't come back for you. dat way it's hard for people to assume dat it was you when his people try and put da puzzle together. They gon think dat it was somebody dat they were already beefing with or niggaz dats from around their way".

"Ok I understand!"

While Chew was talking to Snoop the old school hustler Smooth pulled into the bowling alley parking lot followed by another car. Smooth then exited from the passenger seat side of the car and walked up to the fire exit door. Chew tapped Snoop arm to get his attention.

"Dat dude you see walking to dat door is our money target"

The one guy that was coming in and out of the fire exit door came out the door and started talking and walking back with Smooth to the car that Smooth got out of. They talked for a few minutes and then Smooth left. Snoop tapped Chew arm.

"Now we follow him?"

"Not yet, today is only our first day studying him, we already accomplished knowing one of his places of business and one of his main workers, besides dat, if you haven't noticed, he got another car following him, so it's a possibility dat they're his shooters dats watching his surroundings, so tonight we not going to follow him, tomorrow we start studying a way to follow him without being seen".

"Aight"

"Today is just day one. we got a whole lot more studying to do. It might take weeks or it may take months but it's gon be worth it. Trust me, dat nigga gotta have some m's".

Chew started the rental car up and drove out of the parking lot. It was now almost 3:00 o'clock in the morning and while Chew was driving, his phone started ringing. Chew answered it when he saw that it was Precious.

"What's up?"

"What you doing?"

"Just getting back to Buffalo from Rochester"

Other than Flash, Snoop, L and Dodge Town dudes, Chew had a habit of not telling a person where he was really at and what he was doing.

"So dats why I haven't seen or heard from you today?"

"Yeah been a lil busy today, but it's like you read my mind because I was just thinking about you and wanted to call you but it's so late and by me knowing dat you're a working lady I didn't wanna interrupt your beauty sleep".

"Yeah yeah, whatever Chew".

"For real"

"Well, if I was so much on ya mind then how about you come over here and see me?"

"Baby if dat's what you wanted, then dat's all you had to ask me".

"It's not just about what I want, it's about what the both of us want"

"I just don't wanna make you feel like I'm moving too fast dat's all"

Precious laughed out.

"You got an answer for everything, nigga you not slick".

"I'm on my way, I'll be there in 15 minutes, do you need me to bring anything?"

"Just bring yourself, dats good enough for me"

"Now, it sounds like you tryna be all slick and smooth"

Precious laughed out loud

"Whatever, listen I'm gon slide my house key under da door mat so just come in"

"Aight"

Once Chew pulled up to Precious house, he gave the car to Snoop and told him that he'll see him tomorrow, they gave each other some daps and Chew went inside Precious house. This was Chew's first time ever in Precious house. The house was so big that once Chew stepped inside he didn't know which way to go, so he called Precious phone and asked her where she was at, Precious couldn't help but laugh. When

Precious came downstairs, Chew couldn't believe what she had on. Precious was just wearing a bra and a thong. Chew laughed to himself and said to himself

"Bet you won't get me tonight like you did at the hotel".

Chew followed Precious upstairs to her bedroom. Once they got into her bedroom Precious laid back down in her bed and looked up at Chew.

"Make yourself feel at home".

Chew sat his gun on the stand by the bed, which would still be in arm reach and took off his pants and T shirt, and hopped in the bed with Precious. Precious looked at Chew.

"So how was your day?"

"Busy as usual, and how was yours?"

"It was aight, but it could've been better if I would a seen you today".

"I have some important business to attend to".

Chew placed his hand on Precious thigh while she laid on her side facing him.

"But it's all good, because you're seeing me now"

This time around Precious wasn't playing the tease game. Either it was Chew's body that was turning Precious on or she was just tired of playing games. Precious climbed on top of Chew, and started kissing him. While they were kissing, Chew had both of his hand on Precious butt. It was feeling nice and soft.

Precious then worked her way down to his chest. Now she was in between his legs with his manhood in her mouth. She was sucking Chew off so good, he couldn't help but grab her by the hair and guide her face up and down his manhood. Chew started pumping his manhood in Precious mouth, and she was gagging on it and moaning at the same time.

Chew didn't want to cum so early, so he stopped Precious from sucking him off and got up, and laid Precious down on her back and got in between her legs and started licking on her clit. Precious was now moaning louder and trying to run up the wall while at the same time trying to push Chew's face from her pussy. Chew knew that he had her now. Precious made eye contact with him.

"Come on Chew, fuck me!"

Chew looked at Precious with a smile on his face and was stroking his manhood while looking her straight in the eyes he said

"You want this dick?"

Precious gave Chew a sexy look.

"Stop playing and come get this pussy".

Precious reached for Chews thighs and pulled him on top of her. Chew started kissing her and while he was kissing her, he slid his manhood deep inside of her. It was like Precious lost her breath. To

"Damn dis some good dick".

Precious and Chew had sex for hours in every position. Chew had to come at least four times. After having sex, they both slept like babies.

Chew must've really laid his sex game down on Precious because when he opened his eyes Precious had a cold glass of orange juice and a plate of breakfast already made for him to eat right there in bed. Chew smiled at her,

"Yeah, I must've laid dat thing down last night".

Precious burst out laughing.

"You was aight!"

"Yeah ok".

While Chew was eating his breakfast Precious was sitting up in the bed beside him talking. Chew I need a favor.

"Damn, right after you give me some of that thing you need a favor?"

"Stop trying to play me! I'm serious".

"What's da favor?"

"Next week I'm going to visit my father in PA and I would like for you to come with me".

Chew almost choked on his food, I'm sorry but I don't do federal prison visits.

"Come on Chew, please?"

"I really don't like doing those visits, word up"

Precious started pouting.

"So, you can't do it for me?"

"Why you want me to go so bad? It's not like me and your pops really know each other, and we'll be happy to see each other"

"Because I told my father about you and he really want to meet you. So, I told him dat I will bring you with me when I come back up to visit, he just wanna meet you".

Chew was quiet for a minute, which seemed more like an hour to Precious.

"I'll go with you this one time, but we not going to make this a habit".

Precious smiled and kissed Chew on his left cheek. Chew looked at Precious.

"I hope you brushed ya teeth while you kissing all on me".

Precious playfully hit Chew with her pillow, and they had a playfully pillow fight.

*** Chapter 12 ***

The North Buffalo spot was now doing good numbers. From time to time Kaboom and other dudes from Dodge Town would go over there and knock off a bundle or two, but mainly Jay Jay and Phats were the ones getting all of that money.

When L came into the North Buffalo house, Jay Jay and Phats was in the living room playing the Xbox with their guns all around. Jay Jay looked at L.

"Respect to the gangsta".

"Respect".

L gave Jay Jay and Phats a handshake and a brotherly luv hug, and then tossed a brick of cocaine over to the couch that they were sitting on. Phats paused the game and went inside of the other couch to grab a zip lock bag full of money. Phats then looked up at L.

"Nigga, you heard what Jeezy said, it's all their"

L smiled at Phats, then he looked over to the guns that they had out in the open.

"Ayo, da spot is doing numbers now, so any day da Jakes could run up in here. Stash them guns in the backyard because as long as they don't find no hammers and large quantity of work they'll just think it's a smokehouse since y'all not bagging da work up, when they run up in here and y'all throw da work dat y'all keep in here on the floor, and they find the fiends crack pipes, they not gonna do nothing but charge y'all as smokers".

Jay Jay looked at L.

"I understand what you're saying bro, but I don't feel right without my ratchet being close by"

"Listen man, their whole purpose is the guns. The guns is what keeps them coming back, you can't have no guns in da spot".

"Aight big bro, don't worry about it, we gon stash da hammers outside in the backyard with da work".

"Dat's all you gotta do is just keep getting dis muthafucking money, na mean"

"Yeah, I hear you big bro"

L gave them some daps and left out the house. While L was driving to one of his weight lic's in Cold Spring, he was thinking about how so much has changed in a short period of time.

Things were going real good, Trina was a fast learner and was on top of her game moving that dope just like L schooled her on how to do, she moved in with L and they were now in a serious relationship.

Just like L told her, she moved out of the house that her and Tyeshawn once shared, got in contact with five of Tyeshawn dope fiends and moved everything through them. Trina took Tyeshawn car to his mother and gave her the keys to Tyeshawn's house.

What Trina and L didn't know was that Tyeshawn wasn't feeling what she did and once he found out about the money she took from him , which was really considered short money to him because he had plenty more stashed away that nobody knew about, he barked on his twin brother Keyshawn and his North Side crew for allowing L to set up shop around their way. So, his North Side crew decided that it was time to get L away from North Buffalo.

While Jay Jay and Phats was bearing down in the North Buffalo house playing the Xbox, three cocktail bombs came flying through the front windows. Once the cocktails landed in the house the fire quickly spread. Phats and Jay Jay took off heading for the back door to get their guns but as soon as Phats opened the back door it sounded like Vietnam.

"BOOM, BOOM, BOOM, BOOM, BOOM, BOOM, BOOM"

The first AK47 bullet hit Phats so hard it almost made his body do a backflip back into the house, he died instantly. Jay Jay turned around and ran into a room that was on the other side of the house and jumped through the window. Jay Jay then hopped the fence and ran non-stop to a gas station and called L to come and get him.

L couldn't believe that the North side dudes had heart to come at them with some gunplay. North side dudes had their killers but they were mainly known for getting that dope game money. Jay Jay was really hurt by them North Buffalo dudes killing Phats, he didn't waste no time at striking back.

North Side dudes was known for being out on their block early in the morning. That was in the main hours for the dope flow money. The very next day after North Side cocktailed L's house, Kaboom was driving a pickup truck down one of the blocks in North Buffalo where they be bearing down at. Jay Jay was laying down in the flatbed part of the pickup truck with the chopper that held 50 rounds.

Once Kaboom pulled up on the group of North Side dudes, Jay Jay lifted up with the chopper in his hands. "Boom, Boom, Boom, Boom, Boom, Boom, Boom, Boom, Boom". Before the North Side dudes could reach for their guns those AK47 bullets was smoking the air leaving two of them dead on the scene and three wounded very badly. The North Buffalo and Dodge Town beef

was officially sparked, it was now official war.
••

Things that goes on in the streets travel fast in prison. Gator was hearing about how his daughter Precious showed up to the comedy show with Chew. With L taking Trina from Tyeshawn and Chew dealing with Precious, the streets were talking heavy about L and Chew. Gator was also hearing about how a lot of dudes were getting rich off the dope game. Gator wished that he was home so bad because a lot of dudes that's eating right now wouldn't be eating as much if he was home.

The comedy show event was the talk of topic in Gators Buffalo circle at Lewisburg. They kept talking about how certain dudes stepped up their game and how they were stunting at the Kevin Hart comedy show. Gator felt that the money was now making certain dudes cocky.

While Gator was in his cell preparing himself for the visit a correction officer came up to his cell.

"Mr Taylor you have a visit"

"Alright, you could pop my cell open"

Gator stepped out his cell dressed and ready for his visit. As he walked down the galley inmates that knew him said "Have a good one".

When Gator got to the visiting room, he noticed Precious sitting at a table with Chew. Gator walked up to the table and gave Precious a big hug and gave Chew some dap. Precious looked at Gator.

"Dad you looking good, what you doing in here? working out?"

"Yeah, I'm trying to keep it tight"

"Well you looking good".

Precious looked over at Chew.

"So, Dad here go Chew, da guy dat you just been dying to meet".

Gator looked over at Chew.

"It's been a long time since I've seen ya pops, but from me looking at you right now, your face refreshing my memories of your pops, you look just like your pops, word up"

"If I got a dollar for each time, I heard that, I'll be rich".

Gator laughed.

"Speaking of ya pops, how he been?"

"He been cooling and taking it easy"

Precious looked at Gator.

"Daddy, how you know his father?"

"Me and ol Flashy Flash used to play ball together"

For the remaining visiting hours, all three of them laughed and joked around. Thirty minutes before the visit was over Gator asked Precious to excuse herself while he talked to Chew. Precious didn't question her father request, she just stood up and gave him a hug and a kiss, then she looked back at Chew.

"I'll be waiting in the car".

"Aight!"

Once Precious was gone, Gator didn't waste no time talking to chew.

"Dat's my baby girl, I see dat she's really into you, just so you know it, I did my lil background check on you, not outta disrespect but I had to know what type of guy my daughter is dealing with".

Chew looked Gator eye to eye as he talked and nod his head in an agreeing way.

"Dat's understandable!"

"I heard a lot about you out there in them streets".

"Well, you know dat everything you hear isn't always true".

Gator smiled at Chew.

"You're right about dat, but for da most part, I can look at you and tell dat ya a stand up brother".

Gator then looked around the visiting room, then he leaned in a little closer to Chew.

"It's like this, I already know what you're into, which kind of reminds me of myself in my younger days out there in them streets. I think I could help you out. Wait hold up, let me be more pacific. How about one of our hands washes da other and together we wash da face?"

Chew looked Gator straight in the eyes with a serious facial expression,

"Spit it out, I'm all ears"

"I got a lic for you, and if you handle it right, I could line up some more for you".

"How much we talking?"

"I'm not gonna send you on a mission for some short change, if I send you on a mission, it's for at least 300,000 and better".

These were the kind of lic's that Chew been looking for. It was starting to sound a little too good to be true, but Chew knew that if anybody could put him on to niggaz with long paper, it was definitely Gator. The question now was could he trust Gator. Now that he's messing around with Gator's daughter, Chew felt like Gator wouldn't be on no funny business".

"Damn, I can go for a lic like dat, but let's get something straight, I don't draw my gun on honest working citizens"

Gator laughed out loud.

"Trust me babe boy, dat's not my style either, I got this lic lined up for you dis Thursday, it's gon be a drop-off with at least 10 bricks of dope to 456 Market Street. it's gon be dis cat named Travis there to receive da shipment, no guns is gon be in da spot, whatever you do just make sure you don't kill him, once you get da bricks, I want you to take it to my wife, Precious's mother and she will make a run and bring you back $320,000 da split is 50/50 for us, you get

325,000 and I get 325,000, you take care of dat nice and smooth and I'll set you out to a bigger one, but understand this, nobody and I even mean my daughter too, but nobody know what we got going on".

"Shitd, I'm with dat, but it's just one thing tho, I'm not with leaving a nigga with long money like dat alive to come back for me".

"I feel you! But honestly dat's not really long money, secondly as long as you is masked up, he'll never know it's you, and trust me Chew if you leave him live, we'll be able to get him again, I got da plug, so I know everything".

"Say no more, I got it from here"

"Dat's whats up"

Chew stood up to give Gator some daps.

"Keep in touch"

"Fo sho"

*** Chapter 13 ***

The cocktail bombing in those shootings involving those AK47's made the streets hot and bought the Feds back out. It was time for L to switch up a few things. L's money was getting longer and longer not to mention that Trina was on her grind as well. With so much heat coming from the Feds L was ready to find him and Trina a house away from the jungle and madness in the streets of Buffalo.

Today L had Trina check out a condo that's in the downtown area by the waterfront. L had to get ready for another Detroit trip. It's a good thing that Uncle Sam introduced L to the plug because ever since the cocktail bombing, Uncle Sam was nowhere to be found and this was strange to L because Uncle Sam always been around. L knew that the shootings and beef with the North Side couldn't have scared Uncle Sam away because Uncle Sam was always use to Dodge Town beefing with other hoods.

While L was on the highway headed to Detroit MI, Jay Jay was back around Dodge Town. While he was on the corner with a group of dudes a black Dodge Charger from a distance looked like an undercover cop car came riding down the street. The block was hot with the Feds coming around, so everybody thought the black Dodge Charger was either the feds or undercover cops.

When the car got close to Jay Jay and the group of dudes that he was posted up with, the back window came down "Boom, Boom, Boom, Boom, Boom, Boom". Once Jay Jay saw the window come down, he took off running. Bullets were just missing his head. As he turned into a driveway, he felt a sharp pain in his leg. One of the bullets struck him in the leg. As the black Dodge Charger was speeding off Kaboom came from the side of the house with the chopper, "Boom, Boom, Boom, Boom, Boom, Boom, Boom, Boom" and Swiss cheese that black

Dodge Charger. Kaboom just knew that he hit somebody in that car.

After Kaboom shot up that car, he ran down the street to check up on Jay Jay. Jay Jay was in pain sitting on a porch.

"Dem bitch ass niggaz shot me"

Kaboom looked at his leg.

"You aight! they only hit you in DA leg, I tore dat shit up tho!"

Kaboom took Jay Jay to the hospital. It was a good thing for Kaboom to return fire with a big gun but shooting back with that chopper only made the hood more hot with the Feds.

When L got the call that North side came through Dodge Town shooting, his blood was boiling. It was now time for him to officially put down his murder game. He couldn't wait to get back to Buffalo.

So far Chew taught Snoop how to lay on a lic and do his homework. now it was time to take Snoop on a lic so he could get the real feeling of it.

Snoop and Chew both was gripped up with their guns on the side of the house to the lic that Gator put Chew on. An hour after UPS delivered to the house, a short dark skin man that looked to be in his late 40's came out of the house walking to the driveway where he had his Ford Taurus parked.

When Chew seen the guy face, he realized that the guy was one of the old school hustlers that he had his eye on at the Kevin Hart comedy show. Chew and Snoop quickly threw on their ski masks and ran up on the guy as he was trying to get inside of his car. Once the guy realized that two masked up men with guns were right up on him, he started to turn around and take off. He only got so far before Chew snatched him by his shirt.

"Bring ya muthafucking ass here"

The guy was scared to death and ready to start panicking. He talked in a loud nervous tone.

"You could have everything in my pockets just please don't kill me".

Chew smacked the dude in the nose with the butt of his gun.

"Shut da fuck up, and if you keep tryna blow it up, I'm gon leave ya ass right here".

The guy grabbed his bloody nose while crying in pain. Snoop snatched the keys from his hand, and looked at the man.

"Give me these muthafucking keys"

Chew looked at the guy.

"Come on, we're going back in da house"

Chew started guiding the guy up to the front door of the house. As Snoop was walking up the front porch he was looking around to make sure no neighbors were watching them. When they got to the front door Chew smacked the guy in the back of the head again with the gun.

"Point da muthafucking key out to him".

The guy pointed the house key out to Snoop. Before Snoop put the key in the lock Snoop pulled out his Glock 19. Chew snatched the man up again by his collar.

"Who da fuck else in there?"

"Nobody!"

Snoop looked at the man again.

"Play games if you want to, and it's gon be a homicide"

They walked the man inside of the house. As soon as they got in the house the guy told them where the dope was at. While Chew search the house, Snoop held the guy at gunpoint and started taking off the jewelry that the man had on. After Chew got the dope, they tied the man up and left out the back door.

Chew liked the way Snoop performed. Snoop went right along with the flow. Snoop couldn't believe how easy it was hitting a good lic like that. Snoop was now turned on to the robbery game.

Just like Gator told Chew what to do, Chew took the bricks straight over to Darlene. Darlene made a phone call and told Chew that she'll be right back. While she was gone Chew went down to his laundry mat and chilled. Gator already had a buyer for the bricks. The person that was copping those bricks was thinking that the bricks was coming Jahid. Gator had it set up to a point that nobody except Chew and Darlene knew what was going on. Darlene's plan was coming along just fine.

When Darlene came back she gave Chew a duffel bag with 400,000 instead of the 325,000. Chew was now feeling like he was really in the loop.

*** Chapter 14 ***

The guy that Snoop and Chew tied up and robbed name was Paul. Paul was a little younger than Gator and been getting dope money for a couple years. Back when Gator was home, Paul was just a small-time hustler but after Gator got locked up Paul started getting some money. When Gator heard about Paul selling dope, he reached out to Paul and started having Paul cop his dope from Raheem's brother Jahid. Paul was one of those lic's that Gator and Raheem used to get their cut off from. At first, he was only getting a brick or two then after a while he stepped his game up to a nice little shipment.

The stash house that Paul got Robbed at was a very lowkey stash house. Other than Paul the only two people that knew about the stash house was Jahid and Gator. Paul was already aware of Gator's shady ways, but for a person that's doing life and still able to make a couple of thousand dollars off him, Paul wouldn't expect for Gator to pull a shady move like that on him.

The next person that came to mind was Jahid setting him up but he thought again and he couldn't come up with a good explanation on why he would want to mess up a good business relationship. Things weren't adding up right. Paul decided to talk to Jahid and check his temperature on his robbery.

When Paul bought the robbery up to Jahid, he was lost just like Paul was. Paul could tell that Jahid was telling the truth. Just like he thought, it made no type of sense for Jahid to set the robbery up. Jahid told Paul that he would check into it for him.

When Jahid bought the robbery up to Raheem's attention, Raheem was lost just like Jahid and Paul. For some reason Jahid had a feeling that Gator had something to do with it. Gator was Raheem man and he didn't really want to come at Raheem like it was Gator that had set the robbery up, but the more Jahid talked about the robbery the more Raheem's mind went back to when Chuck was telling him about Gators ways. Deep down inside Raheem was hoping that it wasn't Gator that set the robbery up.

If Gator did, then that means Gator was not only bad for business but he also needed to be dealt with, because if he did that, that was a foul move that could have got Raheem's brother Jahid caught up in some serious beef. Raheem was very over-protective about his brother, so he felt like it was on him to take care of the problem.

Raheem decided to talk to Gator about the situation and pay attention to his body language to make sure that he wasn't lying because if he was lying and had something to do with it, then he would have to be handled. Gator was now bad for business and moving like a snake on some serious shit behind his back. Situations like this could have gotten Jahid killed and who's to say that if Gator did that to Paul, that he wouldn't do it to Raheem in the long run.

When Gator came to the yard Raheem called him over as soon as he came into the yard

"As-Salaamli- Alaiqkum"

"Wa-Alaykum-Salaam"

Raheem looked Gator straight in his eyes.

"Come on Ock, let's take a spin".

While they walked the yard, they talked to each other.

"You heard about ya man Paul getting booked?".

Gator looked at Raheem with confused facial expression

"Naw, I haven't heard anything like dat, what happen?"

"Boy called my brother thinking that he had something to do with it"

"Why would he think that?"

"Because the stash house dat my brother get it delivered to is a low spot that only you and my brother supposedly know about".

"Dat nigga bugging out, what makes him think dat somebody else couldn't had stumbled over his stash spot?"

Gator was trying playing it off smooth, and shook his head and looked at Raheem with a serious facial expression.

"Tell ya brother don't even sweat dat, I'm a get down to da bottom of dis because dat nigga bet not be trying to call himself being slick and have ya brother feeling like he need to lookout or something, I'm gonna check into this shit, word up!"

While they were walking the yard talking about the whole Paul situation a C.O called Gators last name and din numbers over the loudspeaker to report to the police bubble. Raheem looked at Gator.

"What's dat about?"

"Oh, dat's my attorney visit, I'm about to see what he talking about"

"Hopefully he's talking good"

"I'll let you know when I get back"

****

Before the Dodge Town and North Side beef started, L picked Trina on some information about where Tyeshawns twin brother keyshawn lived at, he kept that information as his ace in the hole. As soon as L got back to Buffalo, he gave Trina his half on the condo for them to move into as soon as possible. Then he met up with Chew and told him that it was time to not only hit Tyeshawn where it hurts at, but also the North Side dudes too. Although things were going good for Chew with him now having a good source for him to get a few dope boys, he was still willing to put some work in with L.

Keyshawn had a nice big house right on the borderline of North Buffalo and Kenmore. Which is a nice area and didn't have any criminal activity going on around there. It was a Friday night and Chew knew that Keyshawn would probably be out partying. Since L and Chew knew Keyshawn always parked his car in the garage and never on the street out in the open for people to know that he lived on that street. The plan was for them to break in his garage and murder him when he pulled into the garage.

Chew and L both were masked up inside of Keyshawn's garage for hours waiting on him to pull up. After waiting for almost four hours Keyshawn pulled into his garage. As soon as he stepped out his Range Rover all Keyshawn saw was the grim reapers. L was the first one to run up on him "Boom". The first shot hit him right in the head, as he was falling "Boom" Chew shot him in the chest. Once his body was on the ground both of them stood over him "Boom, Boom, Boom, Boom". It was one ugly scene. Chew and L's bullets ripped Keyshawn's face and head open. Keyshawn wouldn't be able to see his brother one last time because it would be a closed casket.

When Gator walked into the visiting room his lawyer Paul Makowski, who was considered one of the best lawyers in Buffalo was seated at a table with a big folder. Once Gator got to the table his lawyer Paul stuck his right hand out for a handshake.

"Mr. Taylor how you doing?"

Gator shook Makowski hand.

"I'm taking it one day at a time and yourself?"

"Not too bad, thanks for asking"

"So, tell me something good Paul"

Paul started looking through his folder. "Well as you can see I've been going over your case and I must admit that you do have a high-profile case. These people would do any and everything to keep guys like you off the streets".

Gator was impatient.

"Do we have a fight to get the life off my sentence is the question".

"I see a fight but ..."

When Paul said the word "but" it seemed as if he paused for an hour

"But what?"

Paul pulled out some papers from his folder.

"You see we have a fight but we don't really have a strong fight. The other day I was talking to the D.A".

When Paul said the "D.A" word, he paused again and took his glasses off to look Gator straight in Gator eyes.

"Now I know that you might not agree with this, but it's my duty to ask you this since it's on the table".

Paul took out two pictures from his folder and spread them around so Gator could see the pictures. "Do you know these two guys?"

The two guys that Paul was talking about in the picture were Chew and L. Gator looked at the pictures.

"I don't know them personally but I know of them why?"

"It's this simple, the D.A. is willing to let you get the life off your sentence if you could help us build a case on these two guys, they really want these two guys off the streets of Buffalo, from what they're saying, these two guys are responsible for a lot of murders".

Gator gave the lawyer an evil look. If looks could kill, Gator would have killed that lawyer from his looks. Gator spazzed out.

"Fuck I look like to you, man get da fuck outta my face with dat ratting shit, you got me fucked up".

Gator then threw the pictures off the visiting table. The lawyer jumped up scared to death.

"I'm sorry, I didn't mean to offend you".

Gator stood up.

"Man, get da fuck outta here".

The CO's came and escorted Gator back to his cell.

*** Chapter 15 ***

Chew was at his main house out in West Seneca at the kitchen table bagging up his weed feeling good. Hopefully with this new business relationship that he's building with Gator, he could quickly get a million or two. As he sat there in the kitchen bagging up his weed all he could say to himself was, "I knew it was a good reason for me to follow up with Precious, not only do she got some good pussy, but she got her own money and her father is the connected. I need to get at these dope boy stash". Things were really starting to feel too good to be true for Chew.

While Chew were in deep thoughts, Flash came into the house.

"What's up old man?"

"Old man? Boy I'll take you to the court right now and spot you game point and you still wouldn't be able to beat this old man".

Chew laughed.

"But anyways, I stopped by to have a talk with you, son"

Chew noticed a serious concerned look on his father's face.

"Is everything alright pops?"

"I just wanna have a serious talk with you!"

Flash walked over to one of the kitchen cabinets and poured him a shot of Hennessy then, came back to the kitchen table and sat down. Flash took a big sip of the Hennessy.

"You know dat I never questioned you about things you do in the street. Truth be told, I know that I'm the main reason why you feel how you feel and why you do what you do. I take blame for that and take blame for why your mother is no longer here".

A tear fell from flashes eyes. Chew knew that one day this conversation would come. It was now time for him to hear his father out.

"I see that you finally met Gator. The infamous Gator as I should say. I know that it's some things that both of y'all have in common. Honestly without the drug selling and his jealous ways y'all kinda like the same type of player in the game. Yall both are aggressive and know how to survive off the weak"

Flash then took a pause from talking, and took another sip of Hennessy. Chew didn't say a word, he just listened to his father. Flash looked Chew straight in his eyes.

"Let me tell you a story so you could get a real understanding of Gator. Me and Gator go way back, we played ball together, he had a decent ball game, but he wasn't really nice, he was more of a gangster trying to play ball, this was back when people used to sniff powder like they smoke weed now. I mean mostly everybody would get their sniff on. I used to have scouts coming to our games and when they came to our games, they were only interested in me. Although Gator would have a decent game and put up some good points, they still weren't interested in him. They were coming to the game to watch me. After the games we would go out and party. First Gator wasn't showing his jealousy, he was doing it more in a slick way by giving me lots of powder to get high off. I guess he was hoping that it would take me off my game but I was still doing my thing, so when I went to college to play ball on the offseason, I would come back around the way to party. I can't lie I was feeling like a celebrity. I just knew that I was going to the league so when I came back and partied on the offseason, guess who was always there to make sure I had a good time?

"I'm assuming Gator"

"Right! I'll never forget dis, he was outta powder but had some crack, we use to put powder on our weed and call it a cooley but since it wasn't no powder around he convinced me to put the crack on my weed like we did the powder. At first, I'm like hell no but everybody else was doing it like it's the new thing, so I did it".

Flash shook his head.

"That high took me to a whole another high, before you knew it, I went from smoking it in my joints to out of the stem, dat crack took over me and destroyed me, I couldn't shake it. See, Gator is da type of guy that can't stand to see somebody doing better than him, just ask yourself a question. If Gator already got a couple of millions and was already making money off Paul, why would he line Paul up to you? And trust me, it's not because you're dealing with his daughter, he lined Paul up to you because he was jealous of Paul"

Chew was now wondering how Flash even knew that he robbed Paul in the first place.

"I'm sure dat he told you if you handle Paul, he'll line up a few more robberies for you, I'm telling you son, Gator is no good and once you rob everybody dat he's jealous of, next he'll be trying to figure out a way to get you and I know dat you is your own man and you gon do what you want to do, but I'm just keeping it real with you about Gator, like I said before, I take blame for you feeling how you feel about drug dealers and for your mother not being here, but understand dat da man dat so called helping you, is da main reason for everything dat was fucked up happened to us".

Chew couldn't believe what he was hearing, and he knew that his father was telling the truth. I guess this was that feeling when he felt that everything was too good to be true. Chew was now in a deep thought and felt fucked up. A lot of things were starting to add up.

. . . .

Ever since Gator had his attorney visit, he's been in his cell. Raheem could tell that something was bothering Gator and felt like Gator just needed some time to himself. Gator was on fire for how his lawyer coming at him with trying to get him to snitch. There was no way that Gator could have that snitch tag on his name.

The reality of Gator not ever going home again was now really seeking in, but Gator wasn't ready to throw in the towel just yet, he had one last plan that just might be able to get the life off his sentence and could keep his name out of the snitch bracket. The first thing Gator did was contact Precious and told her to come back up to visit him by herself as soon as possible.

Once Precious got the call from her father, she made it up there. When Gator came into the visiting room, he saw Precious looking all worried. Gator walked up to the table and gave her a hug. Precious looked at Gator.

"Is everything alright dad?"

"Things not looking good baby".

Gator shook his head as if he was stressing, this was the first time Precious had ever saw Gator so down. It was now stressing her out. She hated to see her father feeling like this.

"Well, what's wrong dad?"

"It's not looking good for me on that appeal with getting dis life off my sentence"

Precious put her hands on her head and shook her head in a stressful way

"Oh lord".

"Baby girl, I need you"

"Whatever it is, I'm here for you!"

When the lawyer came in to see me, he had a pictures of Chew and his right hand man.

"Picture of them for what?"

The feds want them off the streets bad, they claim that they're responsible for all of them recent murders, especially that one boy that just got murdered in North Buffalo.

Precious was now wondering where her father was taking this thing about Chew and L.

"Ok, so what dat got to do with your appeal?"

"Since you dealing with Chew, if you could help them lock up Chew they'll knock off da life on my sentence".

Gator figured that if Precious was the one to help them lock up Chew and L, his name would still be good and people wouldn't know that he had Precious do it to get the life of his sentence.

Precious couldn't believe what she just heard come out of her father's mouth. Not the man that was all about honor and principles. Not the man that claimed to despise rats. Not the man that she looked up to as one of the realest gangsters to walk this earth, and last but not least, not the man that she wanted her future husband to be just like.

Just like Gator got loud and flipped out on his lawyer, Precious got loud and spazzed out on Gator.

"ARE YOU FUCKING SERIOUS, ASKING ME TO DO SOME SNAKE SHIT LIKE DAT FOR YOU"

The whole visiting room turned their attention to Precious and Gators table.

"Whatever happened to you being a real stand up man with morals and principles? All dat crap you preached to me about hating snitches, you turn right around and got the nerve to ask me to snitch on da man dat I love? I don't believe you".

Gator couldn't believe how precious just flipped out on him and caused a big scene, he was trying his best to get her to calm down, so the other inmates wouldn't hear what she was talking about. Precious stood up and walked right out of the visiting room. Gator tried to reach over the table and grab her hands so she could sit back down, but Precious was too quick. As she was walking away Gator called her name

"PRECIOUS COME HERE"

Precious ignored Gator and kept walking while tears rolled down her face. As soon as she got outside of the facility it felt like she was about to have a nervous breakdown. The first person she called was her mother.

Darlene answered as soon as she saw the caller was Precious.

"Hello"

"Something is really wrong with ya husband, he had da nerve to ask me set Chew up to the Feds for him to get dat life off his sentence".

"Don't talk like dat over these phones, as soon as you get back to Buffalo just come over and we'll talk".

"Ok, bye"

As soon as their phone call ended, Darlene just smiled to herself said out loud,

"There's nothing like a plan that comes together"

Back when Darlene was in high school, Flash was the talk of Buffalo for his basketball skills. Almost every female liked Flash, Gator was also the talk of Buffalo for his bad boy ways. Gator was young and real deep in the streets getting money.

It was really Flash that Darlene liked and was feeling but at the time she really had a thing for street dudes. Especially if they were getting money. Gator was the talk of school and his name was ringing bells on some gangster shit in the streets. Gator took good care of Darlene which was one of the main reasons why she stayed with Gator.

As time went along Darlene started knowing Gator like the back of her hand, she started noticing Gators jealous ways especially when him and flash started playing basketball together on the same team. Flash use to bring out a big crowd to his games, and the fans use to scream out his name when he put on a show. Darlene witnessed the shady things Gator did to Flash by turning him out to drugs. Truth be told she felt bad for Flash getting hooked on to drugs and messing up his basketball career.

After Gator received his life sentence and Darlene heard about Flash wife being killed in a car accident, she started looking for Flash but couldn't find him because he was in rehab. Once Flash got out of rehab and got himself together, Darlene started hearing about him doing good. Gator had Darlene making a few moves for him while he was locked up. She pretty much knew all the major players in the game and was familiar with the streets.

She started hearing about a dangerous stick up kid in the streets that go by the name Chew. Gator left Darlene with plenty of money which would make her a lic to a stick-up kid, so it was important that she kept her eyes and ears open to the streets.

After doing her homework on Chew and finding out that he was Flash's son who actually was the person to get Flash back on his feet, she started tracking Flash down to get close to him and have Flash help her out with her promotion side of business.

As time went along Darlene started noticing more and more of Gator's jealous ways and wanted to leave Gator, she wanted to just take off with his money real bad, but it was two things that were stopping her from making that move. One, was Precious, she knew Precious was blind to Gators foul ways and had a strong bond with him to a point that she wouldn't understand why Darlene left. The other was because she knew that Gator would have somebody track her down and kill her. Darlene needed for two things to happen for her to leave Gator and be alright.

Darlene needed for Precious to witness her father's foul and jealous ways with her own eyes, so she could have a real good understanding. Darlene also needed some muscle that wouldn't allow Gator peoples to track her down. So, Darlene came up with a plan that nobody could see coming.

Instead of getting the laundry mat herself, Darlene talked Flash into to getting the laundromat, she knew that if Chew had gotten the laundry mat right next to Precious nail shop that eventually the two would start messing around with each other and when they start messing around with each other it will lead to Chew meeting Gator.

Darlene already knew how over-protective Gator was over Precious, and that soon or later Gator would want to meet Chew, and after a while of dealing with Gator, Chew would realize how foul and jealous Gator was. By the time Chew would find out about Gator's ways, Precious would be too deep in love with Chew to side with Gator and would see for herself how foul her father was.

But instead of Chew finding out about Gator ways first, Gator did the unthinkable and came at Precious in a way for Precious to see his foul and jealous ways. Now, all

Darlene needed was for Flash to break everything down to Chew about Gator, and once Chew found out from Precious what Gator tried to have her do, Chew would be pissed off and would no longer want any dealings with Gator, and Chew would eventually make Precious choose a side because if she wanted to keep dealing with her father then Chew would keep his distance from her

Darlene's plan was coming together just fine, now that she was much older, all she wanted was to really settle down with Flash and be happy. This was something that she always wanted with Flash. At this age, the bad boy image didn't matter to her. Darlene was now ready to run off with all of Gators money with Flash, and was no longer worried about Gator having somebody track her down, because Chew was heavy in the streets and wouldn't allow any harm to come his father way. Although Gator wasn't aware of Darlene's plan, it would still be considered some get back to Gator for all of the foul things that Gator did to him.

*** Chapter 16 ***

With Precious getting loud at the visit with Gator it wasn't a good look for Gator. Other inmates were ear hustling at the visit and went back to Raheem letting him know about what happened. The news about Gators visit with his daughter confirmed Gator sneaky foul ways to Raheem. Raheem felt like it was his responsibility to handle Gator and. The things that Gator was doing behind his back was a no-no.

Raheem played things off nice and smooth and had Gator thinking that he wasn't believing the things he was hearing about him. One day while they were in the yard working out he waited for Gator to go up on the pull up bar.

While Gator was doing his pull-up's, Raheem pulled out an ice pick and started poking Gator up. Gator never seen it coming all he felt was the sharp pain he fell off the pull up bar, and started trying to kick Raheem off him but Raheem just kept poking him. The C.O in the watchtower noticed the commotion and gave out a warning to break it up, Raheem didn't stop until he heard a warning shot from the tower. By this time Gator was in serious pain and leaking blood from everywhere. Gator was rushed off to the nearest hospital where he remained in critical condition

Chew was sitting in the living room at his main house in West Seneca drinking Hennessy and looking at some old pictures of his mother. The story that flash told him had Chew really feeling some type of way about Gator. Chew felt like Gator was really trying to play him as a pawn in his chess game of life.

Honestly at this moment Chew wanted to be left alone so he can get his mind together, but when Precious called him telling him that she really needed to talk to him about something that's very important, he told her to come over.

While Chew was in the living room in deep thoughts, he was interrupted by the doorbell. When Chew got to the front door and looked out the window it was Precious at his door. Chew opened the door and let Precious inside of the house. When Chew looked in Precious face, he noticed bags under her eyes like she'd been crying. With a serious facial expression Chew look at Precious.

'What's wrong with you? It looks like you been crying".

Precious sat down on the couch, I just had a bad visit with my father. Just hearing about her father had Chew feeling some type of way.

"What happened at the visit?"

"Never in a million years would I thought the day would come for me to choose sides with another man over my father's side".

Chew was now loss and confused.

"What you mean?"

Precious looked up at Chew with tears in her eyes.

"My father told me dat da Feds is trying to build a case up on you and ya man about some recent murders, and then he had the nerve to ask me to help them build a case on you so they could get the life knocked off his sentence when he do is appeal".

Chew couldn't believe his ears, he couldn't believe that a so-called Street legend was trying to get somebody to cut a deal with the feds to help him come home. As far as the Feds trying to build a case on him and L, he wasn't worried about that because last he checked a dead men couldn't talk, and his circle was solid, so Chew wasn't worried about any of them telling on him.

"Ayo, I don't know what's up with ya pops, word up! Dat nigga playing a foul and dangerous game with da wrong nigga. It's sad how these so called stand up gangsta dudes like him a let da Feds break him down to a bitch ass nigga, word up! I just don't get it".

"Listen Chew, one thing you don't ever have to worry about me doing is betraying you, even if I wasn't in love with you, I would never, and I mean never would snitch on you, to be honest with you I was really hurt to hear my dad thinking about some snitching shit, I really looked up to my father as a real stand up gangsta with morals and principles, and to see him go left on me hurt me real bad, as I was on the airplane coming back home, I realized how much I really love you, I love you enough to turn my back on my father and be loyal to you".

From the way precious was talking it seemed like she was more official than her father.

"So, let me get this straight, you willing to leave your father side to be loyal with me?"

"Let me make this clear, even If I wasn't going to be with you, I would still leave my father's side because how my father is moving is not right at all. What's right is right, and what's wrong is wrong. Yes, I do wanna be with you and if I haven't showed you dat, then I don't know what more to show you".

That was more than enough for Chew to hear. Precious just really showed Chew that she loved him and that she had morals and principles. Chew looked Precious straight in her eyes

"Yeah, I think dat you done showed dat you want to be with me, and honestly, I feel da same as you feel. I think we should make this thing official"

"Please Chew, please don't hurt me, I just wanna be loved"

Chew reached his hand out for Precious hand, and pulled her into him and gave her a hug and a kiss. For the rest of the night they made love.

At 4:00 o'clock in the morning Chew heard a big thump at the front door. By the time he realized what was happening all he heard was FBI get down on the floor with your hands up. It had to be at least 20 federal agents in his house with their guns drawn out. Chew wanted to make a dash to his closet to grab his AK47, but when he realized that Precious was also in the bed with him, he thought twice and just complied with the Federal Agents orders. Precious opened her eyes and couldn't believe what she was witnessing.

While they were handcuffing and reading Chew his rights Precious was asking them questions trying to figure out what was going on. After they hand cuffed Chew, they ransacked his house and found two handguns, an AK47 and 20 pounds of weed. Chew looked up at one of the agents.

"She ain't got nothing to do with anything in this house, she's just visiting"

They didn't arrest Precious, they charged Chew with everything. As they were walking Chew out in handcuffs, he looked back at Precious.

"Contact my father and tell him to get in contact with my lawyer".

While they were taking Chew out of the house in hand cuffs, Precious was crying. When they got down to the County jail and took Chew in the intake unit, he saw L inside of the bullpen right across from him. After fingerprinting Chew and processing him they moved him into the bullpen with L. L looked up at Chew with a smile on his face.

"We made the news bro"

Chew shook his head at L and then smiled.

"Nigga you bugged out".

"I don't know about you, but when they came and got me I was up in some pussy"

L laughed out loud.

"Word up!"

"I just got out of some and was knocked out, they so lucky dat she was in da bed with me because I would have grabbed dat chopper and played it off like I didn't know they were the FBI".

"I swear to God I was thinking da same thing".

"What they knock you with?"

"They only caught me with a half a thing, chopper and my pistol".

"They knocked me with 20 pounds, two hammers and da chopper".

"I wonder what the fuck they hit us for in the first place".

"Man, they don't got shit on us, I don't fuck with drugs so it gotta be about dem niggaz".

"Yeah, I was thinking da same thing they just trying to build some shit on us"

"Man, you ain't gonna believe this shit. tell me why my bitch said dat her pops lawyer tried to get him to cooperate with them against us".

"Get da fuck outta here, I don't believe dat shit"

"Trust me, it's true because instead of him working with dem and fuckin his name up, he tried to have my bitch line us for him to keep his name clean".

"Say dat's ya word"

"Man, dat's my word! my bitch came and told me everything. She barked on that nigga and left outta the visit room, she no longer fucking with him"

L shook his head.

"Dat's crazy how niggaz we once looked up to let these crackers break them and fold them up, word up! Dat nigga is a coward"

While they were talking, the federal agents came up to the bullpen an unlock the door and escorted them to a room. When they sat down in the chair one of the federal agents pulled out a folder and examined a few of the papers that were in there, he then laid some pictures of the crime scene to a few of the murders that Chew and L committed on the table.

"I'm sure dat you fellas are familiar with these pictures".

Chew and L looked at the pictures. Then Chew looked back at the Federal Agent.

"Not at all"

"It makes sense to why you fellas would claim that you know nothing about these pictures"

"I don't know what you talking about"

"I'll tell you what, I'm gonna give you a chance to help yourself"

With his face frowned up, L looked at the Federal Agent.

"And how you gonna do that?"

"You give me some information and if it's valid I can have the judge take that into consideration"

Chew burst out laughing, L looked at Chew with the serious facial expression.

"Chill bro, L looked back at the federal agent with a sad facial expression, then he shook his head and put both of his hands on his head. "I can't hold it in any longer, I gotta let it out"

Chew Looked at L with a confused facial expression. L never look back at Chew.

"Man, I'm a start from the beginning and tell you how it all started"

The federal agent pulled out a pen and paper. Then he hit the record button on a recorder that was placed on the desk. Chew was still lost at what L was saying. This was all a shock to Chew, he didn't even stop L from talking, he just was in shock listening to everything L was saying. L took a deep breath and looked the federal agent straight in the eye

"It all started when we were in our early teens"

"What age to be exact?"

"Fourteen if I'm not mistaken"

The federal agent wrote something down on the paper. So, you guys were Fourteen years old?

"And we were supposed to be on our way to school but the new Jordans had just came out, and back then it was a long line, so you had to get up early and be down at footlocker before they opened up, we got there early, and it was this older lady right behind us in line. I asked the lady could she hold our spot in line while we run up to the food court and get us some breakfast, she agreed to hold us a spot in line and we went up to the food court for breakfast. As we were sitting down eating our breakfast, we noticed this man sitting down eating was staring at us a few tables down from where we were seated, he just kept looking at us. The next thing you know the guy gets up and comes over to us and he got this sad facial expression on his face. He tells me that he just got a bad phone call that his son was just murdered.

It was like the federal agent was happy to get some information from L.

"So, I say to the man I'm sorry to hear about your loss, he said that I look just like his son, which is the reason why he kept looking at me, then he told me about this old saying that him and his son would say to each other whenever they were out in public and offered me a couple of dollars to say the old saying with him. I told the man that he didn't have to pay me, if da old saying will make him feel better, then I'll do it for free"

"Ok, so what was the old saying?"

"Whenever he would see his son in public he would give him a hug and when the father would walk off, he would turn around and raise up his right arm with his fist balled up, the son would do the same in return and say "Ok pops I got you"

Federal agent looked at L.

"Ok"

"So, the guy went back to his table and finished his meal. After he finished his meal he walked back over to us and gave me a hug, then he walked about 10 feet away an raised up his right arm and said ok son I love you. I raised my right arm up and said ok pops, I got you! And the man went his way. Three minutes later a waitress came to our table with a food bill in her hand, she said that the guy that I said ok pops I got you, said that I'm supposed to pay for his food bill. So now I'm upset because I don't even know that guy, and only got my Jordan money left on me, but to avoid the lady calling the cops, I paid the guy food bill. As soon as I paid the bill, me and my bro ran out of the full court to track down the man. I was mad and could have killed ten people".

"Did you ever find that guy?"

"We were looking all around for dat guy, right when we was about to hop on the bus and head to school my bro spotted him out"

"Ok, so he spotted him out, and then what?"

"My bro was the first one on the man but he was no match for the old timer, dat man was more experienced and giving the business to my bro, so I picked up this little bat and started hitting the man in the head with it"

"So, you're beating him upside the head with a little bat?"

"Exactly, I'm beating him upside da head like I'm beating you upside the head with this story"

Chew burst out laughing. L looked at Chew.

"Got em, fuck outta my face"

The federal agent was so mad that he jumped over the desk and tried to strangle L. The other agent had to come in and pull him off L.

*** Chapter 17 ***

The charges that they gave Chew and L was the Rico. They had several charges. Besides the things that were found in their house the charges they were facing was Racketeering, Extortion, Murder, Conspiracy and Robberies. Truth be told they didn't really have any strong evidence on L and Chew.

It was the bodies that made them snatch up L and Chew. The Feds plan was to get somebody to lie on them to get the charges to stick. They knew that the feds didn't really have nothing on them, but they also were aware of how the Feds could be to get a conviction. As long as they remained silent and have their lawyers fight hard, they should beat a lot of those charges. They both knew the consequences to the game that they were playing. It was no stress and just part of the game to them

When they got to their units the first thing, they did was make a few phone calls.

Just because they were locked up, the game didn't stop. It was now time to set up shop in jail and get money from the inside, they were going to have Snoop and Jay Jay bring them a mother-load of drugs. Drugs is what control most jails. They were going to get as much of it as they could. The first person Chew called was Precious, he had to make sure that everything was straight with his house.

Precious quickly answered.

"You have a collect call from an inmate at the Erie County Correctional Facility to accept the call press #3 Precious pressed #3 as soon as the operator said to press 3 to accept the call.

"Chew what took you so long to call me?"

"It took them a minute to process me"

"Well, I talked to your father and we talked to your lawyer, I told your father that he don't got to be worried about doing everything himself and that I'm also here for you"

"Listen I'm gon be down for a long time fighting this case and I know dat you got a life of ya own, so I'm not going to be stingy and try to hold you up and have you riding this thing out with me".

"Hold up right there, the other day when I told you that I love you and dat I'm with you I meant every word dat I said. I understand that you're in a situation dat's serious, but dat's when you'll see people true sides. I'll show you better than I'll tell you, this is nothing new to me, I've been down this road with my father up until he came at me with dat bullshit. I was with him every step of da way, when I love a person, I love hard and I love you, I'm here for you and I'm riding this bid out with you, all I ask is dat you put ya trust in me and marry me"

Once Precious mentioned the Mary part to Chew, he was lost for words. Usually it was a man asking a lady to marry him, but Precious was asking Chew to marry her. This was a big step for Chew at a crazy time, he didn't know what to expect".

"Let me ask you a question, why you feeling me so much?"

"My mother once told me that in life you're gonna come across three Good men. One of them is gonna come at a time in your life when you're still learning and you're gonna take it for granted by not understanding it value. sometimes we don't realize love until it's gone. The second one is gonna come at a time dat you're too busy trying to hold on to the first love dat you're not gonna realize it, when you do realize it you're gonna let it pass you by because he's not ya type, us females got a habit of not dealing with da ones dat love us for da one dat just like us because da one dat love us is not really da one that we like, and da one dat just like us is da one dat we really love, then it's da third one, which is da one dat we like and love everything about, but it takes some striving to get and if you let da striving part get in da way of getting him because it's plenty of other guys dat you can have, you'll lose him, at this point in my life I realized dat you're dat guy and I don't wanna lose you".

"Damn baby dat's deep, I think we gotta sit down face to face to talk about this more in person".

"I'm cool with dat, ya lawyer supposed to be coming up there to see you sometime today and ya lil brother Snoop said dat he gotta come and see you, so I'm gon let them have today and come up and see you tomorrow morning".

"Ok, dat sound like a plan".

"Don't worry about nothing, this phone will always be on and I'm gonna make sure dat your account stays right, all you need your father for is to handle ya business, I got everything else. It's now my job to make sure dat you stay right".

"I hear you talking"

"Give it some time and I'll show you better then I'll tell you"

        On the other phone L was talking to Trina.

"What's up sexy?"

"With all this going on you still got a sense of humor and know how to make me smile. Just hearing ya voice alone got me smiling. I would have thought that you would be too stressed out to talk"

"I can't let this thing stress me out whatever happens just happen,s I know what it was hitting it for when I first got into these streets. I signed up for this, all I gotta do is fight and try to stay in good spirits na mean"

"It's good to see you holding ya head, you know dat I'm gonna always be here for you"

"dat's how it normally goes for the first two years everybody be around and then slowly but surely everybody fades away".

"Melo I've been with a few guys before but none of them ever made me happy and taught me so much like how you did, just in da little bit of time we shared with each other, I gained so much from you and you became my everything, and this is beyond da relationship, you became my best friend and everything. I will never turn my back on you. It's not enough money or excitement in another nigga dat could ever take me away from you. I'm ya bitch for life through all the dark nights and pain I will forever be ya rider".

"You making dat shit sound real good, word up!"

"I'm so serious".

L already knew how this part of the game went so he wasn't fully believing Trina would be by his side through all of this, but for the mean time he had to roll with her until she fell off. It was like Trina was reading his mind because she picked the conversation back up to what he was thinking".

"I'm not gon sit up here and say dat I'm gon be a saint out here, but whatever happens I'm gonna be dat down as bitch on ya side dat you could depend on anytime"

"We gon talk about our life when you come up and visit me tomorrow"

"Tomorrow? Nigga I'm coming to see you today"

"Yeah, now you really making this thing sounds serious"

"I've been serious with you from da jump".

"Ok, dis what we gonna do today, my lawyer and little Jay Jay gotta come an see me, so we can prepare for this fight, so, I want you to come first thing tomorrow morning and we gonna sit down and come up with something to keep this thing of ours flowing".

"Ok bae, I'll be there first thing in the morning"

"Aight, I'm a call you back later"

"Ok, love you"

"I love you more".

■ ■

The streets were talking about Chew and L's case like it was just over for them. A lot of people was happy that those two were off the streets. Snoop and Jay Jay was also feeling some type of way about the Feds snatching Chew and L up.

Chew and L were really like their Big Brothers they took care of Snoop and Jay Jay. When Chew came down to the visiting room, he smiled when he saw Snoop. When he walked up to the table, they greeted each other with their brotherly luv hugs. Chew looked at Snoop.

"Fuck you looking all sad for nigga?"

"Man, I hate seeing you like this".

"Dis shit is just the part of d game, you know how this shit go. It's either locked up, dead or rich! We signed up for this shit so it is what it is".

Chew looked around the visiting room, then he leaned in more towards Snoop.

"Me and L been schooling you and Jay Jay since y'all first jumped off da porch. It's Time for y'all to step y'all game up and take this thing of ours to da next level. It's your turn baby boy. I left you with da plug and with enough game to survive with. Now it's time to put all those jewels dat I gave you to work, this shit ain't never going to stop, just like I took care of you and gave you da game, you do the same with the next lil nigga, dat's how we plant our seeds and keep our cloth authentic, keep this shit flowing, don't worry about me, I'm gon stand tall and fight these peoples I just need for you to be focus"

The conversation that Chew was having with Snoop was motivation to Snoop

"Shitd, nigga I'm focus, you ain't gotta worry about me fumbling. I just wanna make sure dat you alright".

"Nigga I'm good! As long as you is out there winning, I'm still winning because you my lil bro, so you is my reflection, rep dis shit to da fullest and keep our shit pure!"

"You already know"

"Ok, check dis out, I don't know too much about da evidence dat they got on me and L, so for the mean time I want you to fall back for a minute, close up da weed spot and get low for minute."

"Copy"

"I want you and Jay Jay to flood Me and L every week with da same mother-load, we setting up shopping in here!"

"I got ya mother-load right now".

"Good! Listen up, I need you to hold my bitch down to make sure she and pops is good out there".

"You ain't gotta tell me dat bro, dat's mandatory! I got all of this, all you gotta do is fight da case and get dat money from da inside and me and Jay Jay go control dis shit out here. Trust me, I got this nigga. Part 2 starts with me and Jay jay!"

The North Buffalo house getting cocktail was a wakeup call for Uncle Sam, he checked himself into a rehab and came back sober and like the hustler that he once was, Uncle Sam made a promise to himself that he'll never get high again and so far, he kept that promise. Uncle Sam was now heavy into the dope game and getting money again. Uncle Sam was now schooling Jay Jay and Snoop to the hustle game.

THE END

Made in the USA
Columbia, SC
26 June 2023

19182016R10189